Cove House

Bristol Bay
Book One

Christine Gordon

August Daughters Press

ISBN 978-1-7326947-3-6

May your first step be a leap of faith...

CHAPTER ONE

Megan Atwood stood at her kitchen sink, staring out through the window at the little box-shaped houses in her neighborhood. She loved this time of the day, the moments right before dawn when everything was dark and quiet and she could leisurely drink her coffee. And just like every morning, the lights began popping on. First, it was the baby's room at Annette's house. Then, the kitchen light at Marsha Jeffrey's house until the entire block was popping with lights. Megan pointed at each house and whispered the names of all the new babies.

How long had it been? She tried hard to divide the years, making sure they added up to sixteen. Almost fourteen years in the city and now, two years of dubious distinction in the suburbs.

They'd come here on purpose. It was a starter

house in a starter neighborhood, full of pregnant women and new mothers with boisterous fathers. And it was flush with newborns and toddlers. It was perfect for them. Except that no matter how much they tried, they always stood out. Not because they were more fit or because they were well-rested. Not because their yard was greener and better manicured. And definitely not because their cars were always sparkling clean. Because no one ever noticed any of those things. They stood out because they didn't have children.

Of course, they were invited to every birthday party, every christening, and countless gender reveals. It was a blur of pink streamers, blue balloons, baby showers, and bassinets. Then, as families welcomed their second or third child, they moved on to a different neighborhood with bigger houses. But nothing was ever lost; There was always another new young couple to take their place.

Megan sighed and pulled the blinds closed. They never should have given a name to it. The little starter house was always headed for failure because it implied that they were going to be moving on to something else, something bigger. Someplace better.

She tried to take another sip of the gas station coffee but it was cold now and left a bitter taste in her mouth. She dumped her cup in the trash and debated if she should dump Steve's coffee too.

It wasn't always like this. Megan had found her passion for cooking early in life and by the time she was eighteen, she was headed off to the best culinary school in New York City.

She met her husband, Steve, only six months into her new job as a sous chef. He was part of a rowdy table of men who were overserved and asking loudly to meet the chef. The chef went through the kitchen and pointed at Megan, commanding her to go out in his place. The entire kitchen quietly snickered at the newbie but Megan didn't care.

Just like Daniel in the den of lions, she decided to do whatever was necessary to tame those men. She pulled off her hat, fluffed her hair, and walked to that table like she was greeting the Queen of England. She smiled too much as she went around the table, shaking the hand of every man and letting them see, up close, the determination in her eyes.

There was one man sitting at that table who wasn't drinking. When Steve Richards took her hand, he held it a few seconds too long. Not because she was insanely beautiful but because he was impressed by her confidence. He didn't notice her exaggerated smile or the determination in her eyes because that wasn't important to him. He only noticed that she wasn't wearing a wedding ring.

After that night, he found he couldn't forget the striking redhead and came back every night for weeks, always asking to see the chef at the end of his meal. By the end of the second week, Megan answered his summons by personally bringing him his bill, claiming his waiter had an emergency and left early. Steve got lost in her bright blue eyes and didn't notice until after he got home that she'd used a red pen to write her name and phone number on the bill.

Steve courted her quickly and they were engaged eight months later. Megan's family wasn't surprised and knew better than to object. After they were married, they settled into a beautiful apartment, content with their choices, and with each other.

Everything was perfect until a year later when Steve took her home with him to celebrate Christmas with his family. Steve's brother had babies and his two sisters had babies and since Steve was the oldest, everyone looked at Megan with suspicion. What's the use of having a young wife if she can't have babies?

After years of patiently smiling whenever anyone asked them if they wanted children, they turned to tests and doctors. When that didn't work they decided to take it out of the hands of Mother Nature and let the experts handle it. Back to back in vitro cycles over five years brought out the vulnerability in both of them and left their marriage cracking under the weight of it.

When Megan told Steve that she couldn't try anymore, he took her back to Virginia, back to her family, with the hope that a new town would give them a new beginning. No one could say they didn't try and some might say they tried for too long until they finally lost sight of what was important to them.

The early morning quiet was interrupted by Steve calling from the back of the house. "Megan, I've found a few more things that I need to pack but I can't find a box."

Banging and some noise from shutting doors echoed through the empty house and Steve brought a bundled stack of books and an old pair of binoculars to the kitchen. He looked around the room before dumping them on the kitchen counter. He was still handsome, looking much younger than a man approaching his fifty-fourth birthday. Megan momentarily wondered where he'd slept last night and if he'd had a bed and a shower.

"Your suit looks new. I don't remember seeing this one," she told him. "Are things looking up in the world of finance?"

Steve smiled at her question because he knew that Megan had reached the limit of her understanding of his profession years ago. When asked about her husband, she usually replied with

Wall Street, referring to where he worked rather than what he did. She basically knew he wore a suit and had a secretary.

"Yes, this suit is relatively new. Are you flirting with me?" Steve half smiled at her, enjoying the chance to tease her.

"You wish. I married you before I could learn how to flirt. The suit was just a casual observation."

Megan grabbed an empty box from a pile in the recycle bin and handed him a red marker. "This has been fun but you can stop all that grinning. After you close the box, write your name on it so the movers don't get them mixed up. I know this is an afterthought, but we probably should have hired different movers."

The thought of how inconvenient it would be if she was accidentally left with one of his boxes made her inwardly groan. There was a reason why she didn't want to know his new address. She needed to make a clean break and after she survived today, she'd have the rest of her life to mourn the loss of him and the dream that came with him. After today, she could curl up in the fetal position and stay in bed for weeks, even months if she wanted. They'd both shouldered too much guilt already and given that it wasn't any one person's fault, it was best to move on as quickly as they could.

"Oh, do you want this coffee, Steve? I got two when I was at the gas station this morning. Out of habit, I guess, but we both don't have to suffer. You can take my word that it's pretty horrible."

Steve nodded. "That was considerate of you. Sure, I'd love to have the coffee but I'll have to take it to go. I need to be in the office early today."

Megan leaned against the counter and wished the movers had finished last night. Steve was late at the office and since she refused to go through his personal things, the movers eventually left the truck in their driveway and said they'd be back early the next morning. She'd never really noticed before now just how uncomfortable a house was without any furniture.

Steve finally finished with his box and Megan had a fleeting thought that she should find the packing tape. But then, the lack of sleep and the light brown coffee only gave her the ability to have fleeting thoughts, not to act on them.

Steve put his box with the others that were littering the kitchen floor. He groaned when he straightened his back and stretched his arms over his head, puffing out his chest and moving around the room stiff-legged. She'd seen him do this peacock strut at least once a day for as long as she'd known him. But today, his blatant attempt to draw her attention was no more than an irritation. She deliberately walked around him to check the backyard for anything they may have forgotten. The narrow strip of a concrete slab that served as their patio was beginning to crack but other than that, nothing had changed. It was still just as empty out there as the day they'd moved in.

"Do you remember how we thought we'd get a grill and do all of the cooking on it?" Steve chuckled. "You said you'd wrap our homegrown vegetables in foil and cook them along with the meat. What's going to happen to your kitchen garden now?"

Megan looked out the window at the tiny square of gray earth that wasn't strong enough to even grow weeds. She remembered how excited she was to finally have a real garden to grow grape tomatoes and make jalapeno bruschetta. And best of all, her homegrown food was going to be so rich in nutrients that her body would miraculously regenerate until she was having two babies every year, a feat only rivaled by the miracles at Lourdes.

"I don't know. I guess they'll either keep it or plant grass. It doesn't matter anymore. The soil out there has too much clay and fixing it would have meant hauling in truckloads of topsoil and then spending years feeding it with organic compost. It was easier to buy our vegetables at the market. I guess it was a childish dream to try to make something grow when it wasn't meant to be. Live and learn, right?"

Steve's face softened when he realized she wasn't talking about the garden anymore. "We came out of this in one piece which is better than most people, Megan. We remained kind to each other and handled everything like adults. We used the same lawyer, we agreed on everything and now we can part knowing we tried to be the best possible versions of ourselves, right to the end."

When Megan didn't answer, Steve continued with his awkward stalling. "You never told me where you were going. For some reason, I always thought you'd stay here, close to your family."

"No, the thought of trying to put down roots again seems tedious. So instead of putting down roots, I'm putting all my belongings into storage. Then, I'm going to just wander the earth. Go wherever the wind blows."

His expression turned serious.

"What does that mean? Does that mean you're leaving Virginia?"

"I'm not exactly leaving, Steve. I prefer to think of it as I'll always be arriving. At least that's what comes to mind when you hear about people who travel. They're always going to the next place. Always arriving, always finding something new. It sounds like an amazing way to live out my life."

Steve observed her thoughtfully. "I don't follow your logic on that. You're only thirty-seven so it might be another fifty years before you live out your life. And I think your mother has always wanted you to come back to Bristol Bay. She hasn't been the same since your grandmother passed. Lately, she's seemed stressed and worried. Maybe you could stick around for a while? I don't imagine your sister is any comfort for her."

Megan huffed at him. "I know you don't like Rachel but at least she went to the funeral. I'm pretty sure she was more of a comfort to Mom than I was, sitting at home, watching you be sick."

"That's not fair, Megan. I didn't make you stay home. And as far as your sister is concerned, I'm pretty sure everyone wished she'd stayed home instead of you. That woman is a disaster and you know I'm right."

"No, you're not right. Everyone expected her to settle down like I did and look at what it got me. I think she's smart about her choices. Just because she's never had a permanent address doesn't make her a disaster."

"We won't talk about your sister then. What about your mom?"

"My mom was prepared when Grandma Coreen died. She was eighty-one and it's not like she had a lingering illness and we all fussed over her for years. She went in her sleep, just like she planned. Sometimes I wonder what it was like when she arrived at *her* next place," Megan admitted.

"She probably already had her ticket and knew

exactly where she was going. That woman never had a quiet day in her whole life. Isn't that why you all called her crazy?"

Megan reluctantly nodded. "Well, you have part of it right. The way the story goes, she was dropped on her head as a baby. She was in her highchair and back then, they didn't have safety straps to keep a child from falling out. She tried to climb out and no one noticed so she went headfirst onto the brick fireplace. After that, whenever a kid was doing something dangerous or doing something that was just plain stupid, their mom would yell at them and say, *You're gonna fall and be crazy like Coreen!* No one ever actually dared to call my grandma crazy to her face. And now that I think about it, she was a little eccentric and bullheaded but I never thought that she was technically crazy."

Steve eyed her curiously. "It just occurred to me that you're a lot like your grandmother. Well, without the accidental fall. Sometimes I wonder what your life would be like now if you hadn't married me. I always suspected that I clipped your wings and if I did, I'm sorry."

"We promised that we weren't going to do this, remember?" Megan pleaded. "I thought you had to get to work."

"Are you okay with waiting alone until the movers get here? And don't forget that the lease on your car is over. You'll need to take it back to the dealership."

"Yes. I won't forget. Have a nice life, Steve. And I don't mean it sarcastically. I hope you find the happiness that you deserve."

He leaned in to hug her. "Take care of yourself, Megan. No twelve-hour days at the restaurant, okay?"

"Sure, I'll be good," she promised. "Don't worry about me."

That was typical Steve, always concerned about other people and trying to be there for her, right down to the very end.

Megan picked up the cup of coffee he left behind and dumped it in the trash next to her cup. She thought about going outside to sit in her car while she waited for the movers but decided it was easier to continue leaning against the kitchen counter

She never would have rented this little box house if she'd known that having a staircase or even a few steps were going to be so important.

CHAPTER TWO

Megan always thought she'd be happier when her life was simple again but all this space just made her feel small. It's as if she woke up today and realized the world got bigger and had offered her endless possibilities for her future but she'd slept through it.

Which is exactly why she hadn't brought up her recent joblessness. She'd worked at the same restaurant for years, but the passage of time had changed the market, and eventually, the decor and menu became outdated. So when the restaurant closed, she wasn't surprised or even upset by it. She equated it to a mercy killing, which oddly enough also applied to her marriage.

As soon as the moving truck left, Megan locked up the house and threw her key under the welcome mat by the front door. Now, all she had to do was survive the short drive home and she could start her well-deserved nervous breakdown. Bristol Bay was the only place she'd ever called home and even though she'd lived in other places, nothing could compare to the small community nestled against the Atlantic Ocean. Home to her was squishing her toes in bluegrass while enjoying a warm ocean breeze.

When Megan pulled into the driveway, her mom was already outside and waiting for her. Alice leaned over the car and motioned for Megan to roll down her window.

"Oh good, I was hoping to catch you before you came inside. There are some things about Grandma Coreen's estate that you need to take care of today. So go on into town to that law office on Queen Street and ask for Mr. Weston."

Megan shuddered at the thought of seeing another lawyer. Even though all of the details of her divorce were agreed upon before she walked through the door, every second she spent in that room was soul-sucking agony. "I promise that I'll get to it tomorrow, Mom. I'm sure one more day won't matter."

Alice's eyes widened and she clucked at Megan. "No, you have to get there before noon today. Mr. Weston will explain everything to you. Now just go along and do what your mother tells you to do."

Megan gave Alice a sorrowful look. "Okay,

Mom. But I'd like to unpack first and maybe change out of these clothes. And then take a long bath and drink my first bottle of wine. Is that Bordeaux blend from Grandma's winery good this year? I'd love to try it." Megan's mind took a dramatic right turn and the further she drifted from the talk about lawyers, the better she felt.

But Alice was unwavering as she pointed at her daughter. "Uh-uh, Megan. Go right now. I mean it."

Megan clenched her teeth and put the car in reverse. Nothing had changed since she was a teenager but she could suffer through a few days of this by reminding herself that staying with her parents was temporary. Nobody ever left Bristol Bay and if they did, they eventually came back. She was going to be the one that got away. The sooner she got on a plane, the sooner she never had to call any place home again.

Megan easily found the law offices of Weston And Weston but circled the block five more times before she parked the car. She took a second to plan out the next few minutes while she walked into the office. She knew that if she kept her mouth shut and nodded at everything the attorney told her, it would be over in minutes. She'll probably have to sign something but that couldn't take more than an additional four seconds. She might even get back home before her mom had time to open the bottle of wine.

Mr. Weston, a white-haired man well into his eighties, smiled and came out from behind his desk when he saw Megan. "Hello, Megan! Your grandmother talked about you so often that I feel like we've already met. I'm Richard Weston and I was a friend of your grandmother for most of my life. Would you like something to drink before we start?"

This was already a disaster. She must be the only client he had today and now he was turning it into a reunion. "Did my mom call and tell you I was coming? Because I might not even have an appointment. If you like, I can come back later."

Mr. Weston chuckled and motioned for the distraught young woman to sit down. Her impatience and wry observation of the situation reminded him of Coreen. "If you'll forgive me for saying, because I'm sure you've already been told this a million times, but you look a great deal like your grandmother. But to those of us who grew up with her, it's more than your looks. It carries over to your general nature. And that's a huge compliment."

Megan nodded politely and tried to suppress a yawn. "I think I'm here to sign something for my grandma's estate. But I'm not sure about any of this. My mom said you'd explain it to me."

Mr. Weston cleared his throat. "Of course. You must be busy and this is a big day for you. So, I'll get right to it. This will was originally drafted for your Great Grandmother, Emma Jameson, and it has been handed down through the generations with the following conditions. First, female descendants will inherit the property, known as Bristol Bay Farms, when they reach the legal age of 18. All property will be directly held by a female descendant and can not be sold, leased, gifted, or allowed to sit vacant for more than six months. All taxes, fees and other yearly expenses are paid by a trust with a yearly stipend paid on an annual basis."

Mr. Weston's expression turned serious. "And now you, Megan Atwood, have inherited your grandmother's entire estate conservatively valued between eighty and ninety million dollars."

Megan sat entirely too still, blinking rapidly and trying to breathe. She swallowed to force back the hard lump in her throat. Tears stung her eyes and her only thought was that she had to get out of there. "Can you explain this in, well, words I'll understand? Or I can come back later. That would probably be the best for both of us."

"I understand completely but this will be over before you know it. In simple words, you inherited twenty thousand acres of prime coastal land. Nine thousand acres of your land is in a high state of cultivation with farmland to grow crops, orchards, a vineyard, a winery, and fields for grazing. Then you have another eleven thousand acres of hardwood timber that can never be harvested. You also have houses, barns, corrals, cars, trucks, livestock, and other outbuildings. And the farm machinery of course. It would be simpler to say that you own twenty thousand acres, everything on it and everything that is produced on it. You provide a good living for all the people who work for you so it's in their best interest to keep the farm profitable."

Mr. Weston paused for a minute, hoping that Megan wasn't getting overwhelmed. He remembered how Alice had reacted when he'd given her the same news six months ago. Still grieving the loss of her mother, it was hard for her to come to terms with the fact that Coreen had kept so much from her. And as much as Alice wanted to carry on the legacy, her husband's health was precarious and she ultimately had to decline. Now Alice would need to help Megan through the transition.

"Megan, all of this is held in trust for you. If you want to know more about the businesses being run on Bristol Bay Farms you should talk to your Uncle Logan. He's in charge of the money. As the CFO, he keeps track of the profitability of each operation. He knows how to access capital funds and diversifies to keep the money spread out. He makes sure that if one part of the farm's operation fails, the others will keep everything afloat. He invests in the stock market, other new businesses, and local charities. Logan also keeps an eye out for any new markets you can serve. If you have questions about that or if you want to see the list of charities you sponsor, they're all on your company's website."

"Bristol Bay Farms has a website and sponsors charities? So the farm helps other people besides the people who work there? Why didn't I know anything about this? I doubt that it's a secret, right?" Megan asked.

Mr. Weston took a deep breath. "There wouldn't have been a reason to tell you about these things before now. It's my understanding that you've been doing what all young people do. You've been living your life. No one expects more than that from you. And you should continue living your life. This shouldn't change anything for you, in fact, it should make everything better, maybe even easier for you."

Megan tried to speak but knew nothing intelligible would come out of her mouth so she just asked, "Why?"

Mr. Weston nodded. "Why just the female descendants? That's an excellent question. The women in your family tend to outlive their husbands by twenty years or more, making the property better held by wives and mothers. This trust has been handed down like this since your great-grandmother, Emma Jameson was widowed. She wanted to make sure that her daughter would never have to face an uncertain future. The lineage started with her and went on through your grandmother Coreen and then to Alice and now you. If the land hadn't been held in trust all these years, it would have been divided twenty times by now, diminishing its worth to nothing. So as long as it stays intact, everyone has a good job and makes good money. Everyone wins."

Megan shook her head in disagreement. "But my mom's brothers and my cousins have been working on that farm their whole lives. What did you tell them?"

Mr. Weston shrugged. "Nothing. They aren't included in the trust."

His words shocked Megan. There were going to be a lot of relatives who were going to wonder why she was chosen by her grandmother to take over Bristol Bay Farms. She'd never worked there or spent one day at the farm after she left for New York City and now she's supposed to just show up and start giving orders?

Megan's heart was beating hard against her chest. "So they know nothing about this? Aren't they going to get angry when they find out they've been disinherited? And worse, when they find out about the will?"

Mr. Weston set his jaw and shook his head. "No one other than the three of us can know. There's a very good reason for that. With the amount of wealth, it's reasonable to expect a certain amount of risk to the woman who stands to inherit this estate."

He took one look at Megan's face and knew he was losing her. She was already mentally retreating and making nervous glances at the door.

Mr. Weston cleared his throat. "Hypothetically speaking, of course, because with all these safeguards, no one can know the truth. But even if that did happen, the males in the family couldn't inherit the land so they'd end up with nothing. By keeping the farm operational, everyone wins. If it goes back to the state of Virginia, everyone loses," he assured her.

Megan nodded but didn't completely understand his words. "I have one question. You keep using the word *your*, as in *your* money, *your* land, *your* winery. Like it's all mine and everything belongs only to me. My mom's whole family works on the farm in one way or another and it supports half the town. I'm sure there has to be someone else, someone more qualified. I'm just not able to take on anything new right now. Besides, that's an incomprehensible amount of responsibility for someone who's never been in charge of anything."

Mr. Weston took off his wire-rimmed glasses

and set them down on the papers in front of him. "Coreen thought ahead and realized that this might happen if Alice couldn't accept her inheritance. She wrote you a letter, just in case you didn't want anything to do with Bristol Bay Farms."

Megan sighed deeply and relief swept over her while she held out her hand. "That sounds great. I'll take it with me and read it later."

"But before it comes to that, I want you to understand one thing. Everything on those twenty thousand acres is yours until you die and your word is final when it comes to making decisions about it." Mr. Weston impatiently shuffled his papers. "If you decide to fire everyone and let the land lie fallow, you can. If you decide to tear down a house and rebuild something that suits you better, you can. You're never going to be dependent on the money that the farm generates because there's money set aside for you to live comfortably, if not extravagantly, for the rest of your life. Your bank book and credit cards are in with the rest of the papers."

Mr. Weston paused, hoping Megan would have more questions, anything to let him know that she was still listening to him. But her face was pale and expressionless. He needed to keep her attention just a few minutes longer.

"This could be a wonderful opportunity for you, Megan. You can travel, go anywhere you want for six months at a time. You can do anything but abandon the land because if you leave for longer than six months, everything will go back to the state. All the land along the ocean shore will be parceled out into individual vacation homes, the vineyard and winery will be bulldozed to make room for whatever tourist attraction will make the most money. All the trees will be cut down and all of the wildlife living there will die. It's up to you."

Megan made an exaggerated show of digging in her purse for the car keys, attempting to stall as long as she could. Right now, she should be watching reruns of *The Golden Girls* on her mom's sofa and polishing off her second bottle of wine. This was the last thing she needed.

"I appreciate all of the time you've spent with me today but this isn't something I can decide right now. So I'll get back to you. How long do I have to think about it?"

Mr. Weston struggled to find the right words. He'd spent a lifetime with Coreen and had just met Alice six months ago. And now, Megan was the combination of both of them; stubborn with a healthy dose of compassion and surprisingly, also quite fragile.

Coreen warned him many times that it would be his job to convince her stubborn daughter to take over the farm on Bristol Bay. And it was with the same determined face that Alice warned him about her kind-hearted but skittish daughter. He closed his eyes for a second and knew she'd probably head for the door if he continued with his stern tone. He lowered his voice until it was a soothing hum.

"There's nothing to think about, Megan. You accepted this responsibility the day you were born. Your mom came in yesterday, on the six month anniversary of your grandmother's death, and signed the papers. She waived her right to the estate and it automatically went to you. As of noon yesterday, you own all of it."

Megan emphatically shook her head until her entire body quaked. "No. But you said it was in a trust, that everything belonged to that trust."

"No, It's *held* in a trust. But in every sense of the word, all of it belongs to you now. Only you," he insisted.

"There's no other way?" Megan hesitantly inquired

Mr. Weston cleared his throat, reluctant to tell her the rest. "Yes, there's one contingency. In the event you aren't able to take the inheritance but you have a minor daughter, the land can be abandoned for up to twenty years. That's in place to give your daughter time to become of legal age and also be able to understand the enormity of her inheritance."

Megan looked down at her perfectly folded

hands in her lap. "I don't understand. You keep saying abandoned like it's a baby or something."

Mr. Weston looked at her with sympathy in his eyes. "You're right. It's just like a baby. Because if you abandon a baby, someone else has to take over the responsibility, not next week or next year, but now. And in your case, the state of Virginia will take that baby, divide it and sell it to the highest bidder. Does that help with your understanding?"

Megan reluctantly nodded. "Yes. I understand what you've told me. I'm a divorced heiress, worth millions of dollars but I can't tell anyone. If I walk away, hundreds of people in Bristol Bay will suffer because of my selfishness. My whole family will be without their jobs and never even know why. So unless I want to be responsible for all of that destruction, I'm the new boss at Bristol Bay Farms. God help me. God help all of us."

CHAPTER THREE

*M*egan stumbled out of the law offices of Weston and Weston, feeling like she'd been held hostage for hours. She'd already exhausted her allotment of patience for the day, what with the movers and Steve, Mr. Weston, her grandma's crazy will, and now her mother was standing in the parking lot waving at her.

"Mom, I love you and all that but you didn't need to wait out here for me. Why didn't you just come inside?"

"Don't be silly," Alice told her in a calming tone. "I didn't want to disrupt your talk with Mr. Weston. Besides, I was worried you'd see me and burst into tears."

Megan didn't try to hide the annoyance she was feeling. "What are you talking about, Mom?"

"Oh, it's just that when you were a little girl

and got sick or hurt while you were at school, you'd start bawling the second I walked into the nurse's office. The nurse told me, confidentially of course, that you weren't normal. She said that children cry at the moment they're hurt, not twenty minutes later. But I knew better. You were too brave to cry in front of strangers. You've always been the strong one in our family. But enough of all that. How are you, sweetie?"

Megan could hardly pull a breath into her lungs. "I don't know, Mom. My body feels all numb. Maybe I need to go to the hospital."

Alice wrapped her arms around her daughter and gave her a long hug. "You're just a little shook up, baby. At least I was when I was summoned by Mr. Weston. And to make matters worse, I was alone with all this information for months. I mean, she was my mother. She raised me and took care of me and all the while she knew what would happen when she died. Why didn't she at least try to warn me?"

Megan sighed. "I think the real question is why anyone would believe what that man told us. Do we even know who he is?"

Alice gave her daughter a comforting smile. "Of course. He's lived here his whole life and he was your grandmother's attorney. Are you ready?"

Megan eyed her mother with suspicion. "No, I'm not ready. You've tried this before, acting like

I know what you're doing. But this time it won't work. I just want to go home."

"Oh good!" Alice's smile lit up her face. "Because that's exactly what we're doing. I went out to Bristol Bay Farms yesterday and it's your turn to go today. If you decide you want to come back to town tomorrow, we can work that out."

"But my car's here," Megan told her while she scanned the parking lot. Realizing that it was gone, she faced her mother. "Where's my car, Mom? It has to go back to the car dealership today."

Alice pursed her lips. "He certainly was smart about not accumulating any marital assets, wasn't he? But let's not think about Steve ever again. You left your keys in the car and your dad drove it home. He'll get it returned."

"And my suitcase? All my clothes are in that car," Megan moaned.

"I managed to get your clothes before he left. So get in my car and I'll drive."

"Why couldn't you do this?" Megan asked her. "Grandma Coreen left everything to you, didn't she?"

Her mother waved her off. "She probably had those papers drawn up ages ago. I'll be sixty in five years and I have your father to consider. How could he keep up his law practice and drive back and forth every day? You'll see. It's better this way."

"But this is all so surreal, Mom. I can't do it," Megan pleaded.

"Yes, you can, sweetheart. I'm going with you and there's not a soul on that farm who would mess with me. Now, there's a nice man who stays at the farm and a cook that comes out every day to Cove House."

"Which one's the Cove House?" Megan asked, her interest growing.

"It's the house where your Great Grandmother Emma lived with her mother before she got married. Her brother was killed in the first world war so it was just the two of them. So sad about her brother. Emma was essentially an only child then."

"The house, Mom? Which one is Cove House?" Megan asked impatiently.

"Oh, sorry dear. It's the big house by the ocean. It has lots of beautiful land and forests but farming doesn't happen there. It's quiet and secluded."

"Did Grandma live there after Grandpa Dane died?" Megan hesitantly asked.

"Yes. I'm a little surprised that you remember Grandpa Dane because you were only eight years old when he died," Alice told her.

"It's only because I just had a glimmer of a memory from that time. Grandma and I were picking apples in the orchard. She pointed to the sky and I heard a seagull. And I had a sense that we were alone, that he was gone, that it was just the two of us."

"That's lovely, dear. Now, if we can just leave this parking lot, I'll take you to Cove House and you can explore it for as long as you want," Alice fussed. "The way you act, you'd think we had to travel out of state. I'll never understand this aversion you have with driving anywhere."

Megan relented and got in the car, mainly because she noticed something unusual about her mother. She seemed unsure of herself, maybe even worried like Steve had mentioned that morning. It was a subtle change, but then her mother was the original chameleon. She could deftly blend into any environment, indirectly influencing everyone around her. But she could also hide there and that's what worried Megan the most.

"You remember Katherine, don't you?" Alice asked. "She's Uncle Logan's daughter and is the closest to your age out of all the girl cousins. I guess she likes to be called Kathy now. No, that changed last year. Everyone calls her Kate. Honestly, I don't understand why anyone would want to keep changing their name. Next, she'll be Kat then Katy. This could go on forever."

Alice huffed a little and turned the air conditioner on high before she continued. "Kate takes care of the house, seeing to it that repairs are made, and does all of the cooking and shopping.

Now there's an idea. You're a chef. Maybe you'd like to help her with the cooking?"

Megan sighed. "Mom, I don't think being a chef is a calling like it is for nuns. It's more like a job that I'm paid to do. I really don't want to cook for a bunch of people, especially when I'm happy with eating some crackers for dinner. Besides, I'm sure Kathy-Kate has it handled."

Alice nodded. "Sure, I can understand that. And then there's Felicity. She's Uncle Bill's only child and a bit of a loner too. She lost her mother when she was a child and has had a hard time of it. She just graduated from the University of Virginia with her master's degree in Fine Arts. She lives at the house but she won't be underfoot. She's very secretive and always runs off whenever she sees me."

Megan choked back a laugh. "Gee, Mom. Do you think that might be because you interrogate her? Maybe she's just shy."

Alice wrinkled her forehead. "I never thought about it that way but you might have a point there. I'll try and leave her alone. Her dad was always too hard on her."

"Well, that might explain her behavior. Especially if she was a little timid to begin with. I'll try to spend some time with her and maybe she'll tell me why she's afraid of you," Megan teased her mother.

Alice regarded her daughter with appreciation. "You were always a strange child, studying people from a distance until you were certain you could trust them. This is going to be so good for you, being around your family every day. You won't need to be guarded or worry about them accepting you."

Megan's expression turned serious. "But Mom, I hardly know any of them. I was eighteen when I left home and my cousins were little kids, running around playing with each other. A few years isn't much now but when you're a teenager, you don't want to play with your younger cousins."

She glanced at her mother, wondering if she should continue voicing all the reasons why she'd never come home for a visit. Even though her parents and grandmother had regularly come to New York City to visit her, it was never really the same between them.

"And then I got married and Steve was always begging to go to his parent's house for holidays. It might seem like I ducked out on my family and traded up for a better family, but it was really quite the opposite. I hated going there. I could feel their pity before I even walked through the door."

Alice nodded at her daughter. "Of course. I didn't mean that you were to blame. And we understood why Steve wanted you to go back home with him to California for every holiday. I just want to help you adjust to your real family here. By now, the rest of the family has been summoned by Mr. Weston and have already received their inheritance. Your grandma had amassed quite a bit of money on her own and that was probably distributed to everyone, along with pieces of her jewelry and other private holdings."

Megan scowled. "Probably? Why would you say that?"

Alice had reached the end of her patience weeks ago and was just barely holding on long enough to make sure Megan's transition was smooth. She'd never felt a deeper level of betrayal like she did when Mr. Weston informed her of the family trust.

He'd told Alice that she couldn't refuse, that it was a precious responsibility handed to her by her mother. Responsibility? It wasn't like she was in charge of the health and welfare of an entire nation. It was just some relatives and people from the town who depended on Bristol Bay Farms for their livelihood.

The fact that Coreen hadn't trusted her with the truth hurt more than any physical assault ever could. Maybe if she wasn't so angry with Coreen she might have considered it and tried to carry on the family legacy. But when the anger left, only a dark void remained. She ultimately decided that it was easier to lie about her husband's health and bow out, leaving it all to Megan. And now, it was more important than ever that she kept her temper in check. Because if provoked, everything might just spill out and muddy the waters. She couldn't lose another daughter.

"Listen, honey, you have to remember that I never discussed it with Grandma Coreen. I didn't know about the trust, no one did. And Mr. Weston isn't going to tell me about what everyone else inherited. He's an ethical man. Besides, I wouldn't even dream of asking."

Alice momentarily took her eyes off the road to check on Megan, who was curled against the car door with her face pressed against the window. She looked tired and defeated. "Don't let me forget to get your bag out of the trunk. I had a feeling you'd want to stick around and explore a little."

"Thanks, Mom." Megan stopped worrying about all the things that could go wrong today and focused on what really mattered to her. There was still time to embrace an old-fashioned nervous breakdown. "You never told me how the wine turned out this year. Do they keep cases of it at Cove House?"

NOLAN PRESCOTT WAS looking for a rock. Not just any rock but the rock that marked where his family home had stood one hundred years ago, back when their land had reached from the Atlantic Coastal Plain far into the Piedmont Plateau until finally resting in the shadow of the Blue Ridge Mountains. But that was before the neighbors came and stole it out from underneath them.

Nolan had looked at ten rocks today but none of them was the boulder that was part of the old homestead's original foundation. His grandfather had described it as a giant monolith, sticking out of the earth at least ten feet high, rising straight to the heavens before finishing at the top with a sharp point. And it sat so deep in the ground that it couldn't be budged, not even with a team of oxen. His grandfather told him that the location for their home was picked because of that rock. They'd built their house against it with the hope that its strength would protect them.

Their family's homestead house was larger than most at that time, a rectangle with that monolith rock sitting at the hearth and chimney. Four more large boulders were positioned at the corners. These cornerstones were rounded in shape but much harder than limestone or sandstone, which is why he was so sure that they're still there, sitting on his neighbor's land.

His ancestors had suffered through more than their fair share of unforeseeable misfortunes.

First, it was the war in 1917, and the loss of their young men. Then, the Great Depression forced hard times on the entire country. As farm prices plummeted, farmers struggled to feed their families. While some farmers were losing their land to the banks, others were grabbing the cheap land as fast as the banks could foreclose.

But that was ancient history. The Prescotts had returned and were determined to take back everything that was stolen from them. The land was only part of it. Nolan had been looking specifically for that monolith rock because that was where the treasure was hidden.

Nolan started with satellite images but quickly realized that the area would be covered with a canopy of trees by now. One hundred years of undisturbed growth had fostered a rich stand of trees and other species of plants, making it impossible to distinguish any differences from the surrounding forest.

He researched old survey maps, some dating back three hundred years, but those surveys were crude and mostly inaccurate. The more recent surveys of his neighbor's land showed the exact boundaries of the property and the dimensions and location of all the buildings. The only problem was, according to these surveys, his old homestead never existed.

He couldn't move onto his neighbor's land

so he did the next best thing. He bought a small parcel immediately adjacent to that land, hoping to find the skeletal remains of the house on horseback or on foot. And then, he bought one hundred head of cattle.

He'd pushed over fences to let his cattle onto their land and soon, no one was suspicious to see him riding through an open pasture or walking along a river bed. Over the last five years, they'd stopped seeing him as a trespasser and more of a harmless fool who couldn't run a ranch.

Nolan devoted his life to raising the money, raising his brothers, raising hell, if that's what it took, to reclaim their land. And now that he's so close that he can touch it, he'd do just about anything to get it back.

CHAPTER FOUR

*A*lice turned off the car and carefully put a fresh coat of red lipstick on her puckered lips. Satisfied that she hadn't missed a spot, she turned to her sleeping daughter and crisply reprimanded her. "Megan, honey, we're here and I can already smell the fried chicken."

Megan sleepily opened one eye and tried to wake up. "I just want to rest for a little bit. Please, mom, I'm not even hungry."

"Well, I can guarantee you're going to be hungry as soon as you see the table of food that Kate's going to set out for you."

Megan grumbled a little until she realized that her mother was right, she was absolutely starving. With her mother in the lead, Megan followed through the yard, up the steps to the veranda, and through the front door of the Cove House.

The moment Megan saw the house, she felt like she had as a child. The wonderment and excitement of the days she'd spent here came back to her in waves of images. She'd spent her summers here, playing on the large veranda that circled the house. It was painted a soft yellow now with green shutters and doors. The white veranda was cluttered with chairs and tables and chaise lounges. Pots of brightly colored flowers and giant ferns were everywhere. Megan tried to peek past the side of the house to see the ocean but her mom had already gone through the front door and Megan had to hurry to catch up with her.

The inside of the house looked exactly as she remembered it but with subtle differences. It was still spacious with numerous hand-carved fireplaces, high ceilings, and miles of white painted trim. Thick, incredibly detailed rugs covered parts of the hardwood floors. But Megan keenly noticed that there was more color in the rooms now. There were blue velvet sofas, marble-topped tables, and engaging artwork on the walls. It seemed that Grandma Coreen had been going to auctions or visiting antique stores and filling the house with these unique, really fun, and exquisite treasures.

Megan had taken no more than three steps when she was greeted by one of her cousins. "Megan! I'm Kate. We're so happy to have you here! I put together a little meal for us so if you wanna come to the dining room we can all sit down and talk and eat and just have fun."

Megan was so captivated by her beautiful pink-cheeked smiling cousin that she obediently started following her. She seemed so fresh and young, so enthusiastic and brimming with love. When Kate turned to usher them into the big dining room, Megan noticed her hair was held back in a long blonde braid. She envied her cousin, remembering how she'd been the same way, feeling like she could do everything, conquer anything. The sky was the limit when she had all that youthful vigor coursing through her veins.

Megan walked slowly into the big dining room. The table was carefully set with a starched white tablecloth and napkins, blue and white dishes, and big glasses of sweet tea. Megan knew she was home. In all those years when she'd been away from this place and Bristol Bay, she'd also been away from the friendliness, hominess, and all the good food and good people.

Kate smiled at Megan and motioned for her to sit at the head of the table. "Sit here, Megan. We were just getting ready to bring out all of the food." And then, just as if they were at the ballet, servers immediately started gracefully flowing out of the kitchen, holding their platters up high and circling the dining room, until all of the platters were directly in front of her. Megan hadn't been this impressed since the first time she saw synchronized swimming.

She was dazzled by the food in front of her. There were heaping platters of fried chicken dusted with cayenne, baskets of hot butter bomb biscuits, pans overflowing with pecan topped sweet potatoes, plates of fried green tomatoes, and a vat of pepper-flecked country gravy.

Megan looked at the smiling faces of the waiters and realized they were her cousins. Alice made the introductions.

"Megan, this is your oldest cousin, Wyatt. He's second in charge of the winery. Chelsea is our resident beekeeper and in charge of the ducks and flowers. She just had all of her beautiful long dark hair cut off but I'm sure it'll grow back in no time, right Chelsea? And this is your youngest cousin, Felicity."

Alice looked around the room and noticed that someone was missing. "Wyatt, be a dear and call Luke in to eat. I can't imagine how upset he'd be if he missed this fine meal," she informed him.

Luke must have been waiting on the veranda for an invitation because seconds later he appeared. Megan tried not to gasp when she saw him. He wasn't the type of man she ever had the opportunity to meet while working in a kitchen. He was a ruggedly handsome young man with an easy smile. There was a definite advantage to living on a farm if her life was going to be filled with men like Luke. Even though he was wearing a long-sleeved denim shirt, Megan spent a few seconds imagining him shirtless, fixing his truck while she held his sweet tea.

Alice whispered in her daughter's ear, "You'll want to save his number in your favorites. He's known as *Mr. Fix It* around here. I heard he's amazing."

There was smiling and chair scraping and lots of chatter. Megan noticed that everyone was joining in except for Felicity, who kept her head low, her long mousy brown hair covering her face. Occasionally, she looked up from her plate, her eyes darting nervously at everyone.

After her first bite of chicken, Megan realized that she'd been settling for a life of bland crackers when what her soul really needed was all of this love and calories.

Sitting in that room surrounded by her family, Megan watched as her mother came alive. Her eyes got brighter and she tossed her stylish blonde hair when she laughed. This is what Megan was missing when she was living in the city when her life had been consumed with Steve. She missed the charming traditions of Southern women.

"Oh my gosh, Kate, what did you do to these pecans?" Megan asked in wonderment. "When I bite into them, first there's a sweet buttery smoothness and then they deliver little snaps of heaven in my mouth."

Kate laughed off the compliment. "Oh, you won't find any prepared food in this kitchen. I cook the old-fashioned, healthy way. This is just an old recipe that Grandma Coreen gave me."

Kate was right. These foods that Megan associated with happy memories of Grandma Coreen made her feel less lonely. It was like having her back for a few minutes.

"It's more than that," Megan explained. "You've added to her recipes. Everything you made today is slightly different. There's a crunch, a saltiness, different spices, and a bonanza of textures and tastes in everything you made today. Even your fried green tomatoes are special. They have a crisp crunch and then I'm hit with the velvet tomato inside. Everything is spectacular."

Kate blushed. "I hope you're not disappointed with dessert."

Dessert too? The little voice in Megan's head kept yelling *yay yay yay* until it was hard to hear anything else.

"Sorry, I didn't have time to make a pie," Kate apologized. "I hope you like peach cobbler. Everything's already dished up. I just need to serve it."

Kate nodded at Chelsea and they both started clearing the table. Wyatt and Luke noticed and were quick to join them.

They were barely gone a minute before returning to the dining room. Kate presented Megan with a large blue-flowered pottery bowl filled to the brim with warm syrupy peaches topped with chunks of crumbly sweet crust, and a dollop of vanilla ice cream and sprig of mint added for good measure. Megan savored every bite and when she scraped the bowl to get the last spoonful, she realized everyone was watching her.

"Wow, this is embarrassing. Why aren't any of you having dessert?" she asked them.

Alice answered for all of them. "Sweetheart, you've been eating your entire meal like a starving bear headed for hibernation. We just couldn't stop watching. Maybe you'd like to have more cobbler?"

Megan looked at each of their smiling faces and, in her upside-down world, another piece of peach cobbler seemed like the perfect ending to the day.

"Yes," she finally admitted. "I'd like that very much."

Besides, the only way she could ingest more sugar was if she hijacked a Pepsi truck and drank straight from the spigot. Eating the second bowl of cobbler seemed more like something a refined Southern lady would do.

ALICE LEFT RIGHT AFTER dinner, citing all
the errands she had to run before her husband,
Walter, came home from work. The truth was, she
couldn't wait to be rid of that place and breathed
a huge sigh of relief as Bristol Bay Farms faded in
her rearview mirror.

She'd accomplished a great feat today. Megan
was safely locked in a house with people willing to
do whatever it took to keep her happy. Alice had
been stern with them, threatening their jobs and
livelihood if Megan spent so much as one single
moment of unhappiness there.

No one at the farm was exactly sure who was
in charge, as it appeared that Alice had taken over
Bristol Bay Farms five years ago. Being the oldest
child, Alice had been involved in all the decision
making after her mother had a bout of pleurisy.

But now, Megan was more than capable of
taking the reins and moving forward. Alice knew
that all Megan needed was a boost to her ego and
there was nothing better for that than a steady
stream of men hoping to court her. And there
wasn't a better place to find gorgeous men than
at Bristol Bay Farms. You see, Alice had been
carefully curating eligible bachelors ever since
she heard rumors of Megan's failing marriage six
months ago.

For Alice, Megan's divorce was anything but

unfortunate. The first time she met Steve, she knew that he was going to be trouble. He wasn't confident or engaging or even good looking. And worst of all, he'd found a way to capture Megan's love before her daughter even had the chance to grow up.

Alice read the bible and understood how it applied to marriage. She accepted that Megan would leave them and start a new family with Steve. She just didn't realize that Steve was going to steal Megan from her. From the first day they were married, Steve monopolized every aspect of her, criticizing her and in the next breath praising her. He was the worst kind of man, uninspired, and only happy when everyone around him was failing. If Alice had been in New York City the day that they'd met, she would have moved heaven and earth to make sure that he'd never laid eyes on her precious daughter.

But Alice wasn't without a heart. She'd felt guilty when Megan had tearfully confided in her all of the details of their failing marriage. She listened to every word but never once voiced her opinion. And when the divorce was final, she wasted no time getting back to Mr. Weston and informing him that it was now his job to convince Megan to take over the estate.

Alice was not without certain charms. She reminded him, not too subtly, that if Bristol Bay

Farms dissolved, so would his fat paycheck.

MEGAN HAD SPENT a wonderful day at Cove House and was now getting ready for an equally wonderful evening. After soaking in a long bath, she'd piled her hair on top of her head and changed into one of the nighties that her mother had packed for her.

She wasn't surprised to see that everything in her suitcase looked like something a bride would take on her honeymoon, as her mother believed that unmarried women looked best when they wore less clothes. And now that she was single again, that's exactly what she had. Less clothes.

There wasn't a single pair of flannel pants or a sweatshirt in that entire bag. Instead, there was an overabundance of new lace bra and panties sets, tiny silk nighties, low cut shirts, and high cut shorts. She groaned when she realized that if she lived in a brothel, she'd most certainly win the award for best dressed in the line of duty.

Her mother didn't see it that way. She saw clothing as a gift, given to women so they could show their light, something the bible referred to when warning young women about not hiding their light under a bushel basket. Many times she'd chide her daughter with the passage, *"there is nothing hidden except to be made visible."*

When Megan was younger, she'd asked their pastor if that was the correct interpretation of her mother's favorite bible quote. He'd turned crimson red and said something about an emergency. Apparently, God sent a broken pipe to the chapel basement and he had to stop the flooding. She'd finally concluded that her mother was right and never bothered him again.

Megan sat in Grandma Coreen's big wingback chair, like she always had, hugging her knees. She looked around the room and remembered playing in here, watching as her grandma did her bookkeeping. Grandma Coreen was always sitting at her desk and now Megan knew why; she was in charge of the whole of Bristol Bay Farms, left to her by her mother, Emma. Grandma Coreen was an only child so she didn't have brothers and sisters to help her. Megan was lucky to have so much support right now.

As the minutes ticked by, she realized that she'd never be able to go to sleep with all these thoughts and memories bombarding her. She pulled a blanket off her bed and wrapped it around her shoulders before she headed downstairs. The dining room and kitchen were clean, without a single trace of their meal earlier that day. But she didn't care about that. She wasn't hungry; she was looking in the pantry for the stash of wine from their winery.

The labels dated back more than ten years so she picked an assortment of bottles, in case a thirsty wanderer ended up on the veranda and wanted to have a glass of wine with her. Then she walked to the veranda, dropping the blanket before she got outside. It was a warm night and everyone was asleep but her. She could just relax on the cushioned lounge chair and watch the full moon rise over the Atlantic ocean while she sipped her wine in peace.

CHAPTER FIVE

The fact that Megan woke up before dawn to the soft kisses from cow lips isn't what made her angry; it was the total destruction of the beautiful flowers in the gardens and on the veranda.

That black and white cow had used her yard as a buffet and then walked up the steps to the veranda and leisurely munched on all the beautiful flowers and potted plants. When he ran out of food, he simply walked over to the sleeping Megan and proceeded to nibble her neck, her ear, her arm, searching her whole body to see if she had any flowers on her. She woke in the dark screaming and fighting off the large intruder. All that screaming alerted Luke.

He arrived breathless and shirtless, finding Megan underneath a wicker loveseat. "I heard a noise. What's the matter?" he anxiously asked.

She looked up at him from her hiding place and motioned to the cow. "I think someone's lost and I'm not ready to give him directions. He's already been more than a little fresh with me."

Luke took a few seconds to process her words. "Oh, you mean Romeo? He's harmless but he sure likes the ladies."

Megan regarded Luke impatiently. "Yes, I'm a first-hand witness to that. But what's he doing on the veranda?"

"He comes around here almost every night to look at the ocean and then stays for breakfast. He's on the veranda because that's where we keep the dessert. He loves flowers," Luke admitted.

Megan fumed. "Can you just...put him back in the barn and make sure to lock him in? I can't imagine why anyone would keep letting him out."

"But he's not ours," Luke insisted. "He belongs to the ranch just west of here. There must be a break in the fence that we haven't found yet. Either that or they're letting him out. Or the third possibility is that he knows how to open the gate. And I wouldn't put that past him because he's really smart," Luke told her with a half-smile.

Megan climbed out from under the loveseat and tried to straighten her nightie. "He comes and does this every day? I would think Chelsea would be furious every time he came over here and ate all of her flowers. Look at everything he destroyed."

Luke's expression turned serious. "Well, I have to admit that Chelsea's not exactly a huge fan of Romeo. But she has a tender side and I've seen her feeding him many times. Maybe you should talk to her about it?"

Megan tightened her lips until they formed a straight line. "No, this is ending today. There's no way I'm going to put up with some cow named Romeo bullying us and coming onto our land and eating everything in the garden, plus all these beautiful flowers. I realize that I keep going on and on about the flowers, but darn it, they're more beautiful than any flowers I've ever seen and now he's eaten all of them." Megan sobbed a little every time she looked at the spilled dirt and mangled stems.

Luke motioned to a truck parked by the barn. "I still have the trailer hooked up to the truck from yesterday so I can just take him back right now if you want."

Megan shook her head at him and gritted her teeth. "Yes, but I'm coming with you this time. I'll make sure he never gets back on this land again."

Luke grabbed a potted plant and lured Romeo off of the veranda. Megan watched with fascination as Luke gently admonished Romeo while guiding him to the waiting trailer. This was already a crazy week and now she was going to return a cow, something she'd never thought she'd live to say much less do. While Luke was closing the trailer door, Megan rushed into the house and grabbed the first thing she saw from the coat rack and then grabbed a pair of boots off the veranda. She ran after Luke and caught up with him just as he was just getting ready to pull out.

"Come on, Luke, let's go and rustle some cattle!" she excitedly told him as she climbed into the truck. When she realized that she still might be slightly intoxicated from last night or even still in shock from yesterday, she lowered her voice, trying to sound serious. "No, really. I know that this is the opposite of rustling cattle. We'll calmly take Romeo back to that ranch and recommend that they get him a shock collar. I had a neighbor with this exact problem and they were able to keep three full-grown German Shepherds from running away so I'm sure it will work on one dumb cow."

Luke shot her a worried look then decided to keep his eyes on the road. He had a feeling that she wasn't the kind of woman who'd like being told what to do. So he decided just to do exactly as she said, even if she sounded a little crazy.

They arrived at the Prescott ranch twenty minutes later. Several men turned to look at the truck when they pulled in and then they went back to their business. Apparently, they were used to seeing Romeo being returned like this every day.

Their indifference fueled Megan's rage. "Who are these ranchers? Do you know anything about this place?"

Luke hesitated to say anything but decided to tell the truth. "They're the Prescotts, three brothers that bought this ranch about five years ago. Don't know much about them other than whenever our fences are down, they're always there, grazing their cattle on our land."

Megan scowled. "On our pasture land? So you're saying that they've been grazing their cattle on our land for the last five years? Isn't there a law against that?"

"I'm not sure. Well, one thing I've noticed is that our fences keep breaking down. But only the fences for the pastures that they use for grazing. And as soon as someone notices the break in the fence and we go to fix it, they've already moved their cattle to another one of our pastures. It's one of those never-ending things that can bog down a farm and hamper productivity."

"You're sure? It's really been going on for five years?" Megan questioned him.

Luke looked down and then finally admitted, "Yes, it's been going on ever since they moved in over on that small ten-acre parcel of land next to Bristol Bay Farms. I took a class in animal husbandry so I know that since they have one hundred head of cattle, they can't raise their grass-fed cattle on just ten acres. It would take two hundred acres, minimum, to raise that much cattle and call them grass-fed."

Megan was quiet. "Could they be grazing on land somewhere other than Bristol Bay Farms?"

Luke shook his head. "No. Their land is locked in on all sides by us. And the only reason why nobody wanted that land is that there isn't any water on it. Well, there's enough water for a well but not water for the cattle. And they can't move the cattle every day in trucks. It's just not feasible."

Megan nodded in agreement. "Have they ever asked to lease our land?"

Luke shrugged. "I don't think so. It would cost more than sixty dollars an acre. That's sixty times one hundred ninety acres times five years. That's fifty-seven thousand dollars. I don't think their operation is that lucrative yet. It's easier for them to let their cattle wander onto our land and claim they didn't know about it and then just do it again. I think your grandma got to the point where she thought it was easier to ignore it."

"Well, I'm not Grandma Coreen and I'm not going to put up with this." Megan liked the sound of fifty-seven thousand dollars. She wasn't sure if she could legally enforce it, but she was ready to at least scare them. She doubted they'd want a lawsuit.

Luke parked their truck next to an old tour bus

from the seventies and hopped out, coming around the other side to help Megan. The rubber rain boots that Megan had grabbed were too big on her and her feet slipped around in them, making each step clumsy and exaggerated. She started trying different ways to maneuver in the boots and then resigned herself to half skating, half pushing her feet in them. She finally made it around the front of their truck with Luke right behind her, carrying her jacket and trying to put it on her. She didn't stop until she flagged down a man dressed as a cowboy.

"Excuse me, but who's in charge here?" She demanded. The cowboy smirked as Luke tried to pull one of her arms into the jean jacket.

"I suppose you mean Nolan. He's in the barn," he said while pointing to a little gray building.

Megan dismissed him with a nod and struggled with the jean jacket. The more she tried to close it in the front, the more cleavage pushed out.

Luke sighed in resignation. "That jacket looks like it's gonna be too small no matter how hard you pull on it. It's on you as good as it can ever get. Do you wanna go look in the barn for the Nolan feller?"

"Oh, Lord, do we have a choice? Maybe we should just take Romeo back with us and, and, you know, keep him,'" she stammered.

"I don't think we can keep him. I'm sorry but he's got to stay here," Luke reluctantly told her.

"Fine. Let's go then. I'm not familiar with barns so just don't leave me in there, Luke. You have to promise me." Luke gave her a reassuring look and they trudged forward to the barn.

Before they could go into the barn, another cowboy rushed past them. Megan grabbed his arm to get his attention, "Excuse me. I don't know who you are, and I don't care who you are, but we have your cow, and he's in that trailer back there, and I want you to get him out and put him in behind one of these fences you seem to have everywhere and keep him off our land."

"I don't know what you're talking about, ma'am, but he can't be a cow. You're probably talking about one of the bulls."

Just then, another man in a cowboy hat called from the barn door, and the man she was holding pulled his arm free. "We'll get to it in a minute ma'am. It's just that they need me more in there. We have a cow that's fixin' to have a calf. She's a first calf cow and she's in trouble."

Megan tied her hair back in a knot, ready to help, and followed the young cowboy into a barn. She stayed behind him until she got a good look at what was ahead of her. And once she saw it, there was no way to unsee three men pulling a calf out of a cow.

Megan leaned back against Luke and tried to take big breaths, cursing all the wine she drank the night before. That's when she saw the calf land with a thud on the barn floor.

Luke patted her back, "I think the worst is over. Maybe we should go now." Megan nodded in agreement and gratefully accepted his help when he put his arm around her.

One of the men walked toward Megan, taking his hat off as he approached her. "Are you the lady with our bull?" He smiled, giving her long full body looks. "I'm Nolan Prescott and who might you be? I think I'm gonna call you Red because you look like there's a fire in your eyes and your hair's as red as any fire I've ever seen."

Megan narrowed her eyes, lifted her face, and leveled her pointed finger at his nose. "I'm in charge now and all this crap is going to stop. You need to keep your freaking bull off of my land. He would've gone through the front door if it was open and who knows what he would've wrecked. As it is, he ate everything in his path."

Nolan Prescott took a step back from the beautiful woman in his barn. Sure, she was dressed oddly but he didn't mind seeing the entirety of her long legs. This had to be the new owner of Bristol Bay Farms. In the six months since the death of Coreen Michaelson, no one had heard anything about who was taking over the farm. People in town had speculated that it was going to be Alice Atwood, as she was the oldest sibling in that family. But now it looked like the old lady had left everything to her granddaughter instead.

Nolan could feel the winds changing, and with that change, his luck was changing too. His charm wouldn't have worked on the grandmother or even the mother. But he had a fighting chance with the granddaughter. He might have to use everything in his arsenal to seduce this woman, but when he looked at the fire in her eyes, he knew that it was going to be worth it. This just might be fun, maybe the most fun he'd had in years. It might be classified as work but he was going to enjoy every minute of it.

They were interrupted by one of the men who were still with the cow.

"Nolan, it doesn't look like this calf is going to be able to stand. Her legs are crooked and she's too small. Maybe just forty pounds."

Nolan nodded in agreement. "Do what you have to do and make sure the cow is okay and the afterbirth is out. I don't want her getting some kind of infection."

He turned to Megan, took her elbow, and tried to lead her out of the barn but she jerked her arm away and faced him. "What was he talking about? What needs to be done with that baby calf?"

Nolan gave her a reassuring smile. "Now, don't you worry about that. We're in the cattle business and we know what we're doing. It's the best for everyone, including the calf. It's just not going to make it."

Megan felt her eyes burn. "You can't do that, you can't just kill a baby because it's not standing like you'd want. Isn't there something you can do for her?"

Nolan shook his head. "No ma'am. There isn't a single thing that will fix that calf now. Doing this is the kindest thing for her."

Megan cocked her head and frowned at him. "What do you want for the calf?"

Nolan regarded her with uncertainty. "I don't understand. The calf's not for sale."

"Really?" Megan retorted. "Because Luke is a savant when it comes to animal husbandry and numbers. Tell the man what he owes us, Luke."

Luke stuck out his chest and stepped forward until he was inches from Nolan's face. "You've been grazing your cattle on her land for the last five years. That's sixty dollars times one hundred ninety acres times five years. That's fifty-seven thousand dollars. And she's not even going to add on extra for all the water you stole. She wants the calf...and that bull we have to return to your ranch everyday...and that old tour bus in return."

Megan smiled. This was turning out far better

than she'd ever imagined. She came here to return a bull and was leaving with that same bull, a newborn baby calf, and a fantastic tour bus.

She was going to continue to use all of her weight to lean the necks of her unruly neighbors until they sat up and took notice; there's a new redhead in town.

CHAPTER SIX

Megan walked into the kitchen where everyone was busy with breakfast. "We have an unexpected addition to our family here at Cove House," she announced to her cousins. "Who wants to help Luke in the barn with a new calf?" She wasn't expecting a volunteer, so she wasn't surprised when the room fell quiet. But then she noticed something peculiar. All eyes slowly drifted to Felicity.

"I could help," Felicity told Megan in a soft voice. She stood tall and faintly smiled with a dreamy look in her eyes.

"Well, I guess that's settled," Megan happily told them. And everyone went back to talking and eating.

"Are you hungry, Megan?" Kate asked while spooning scrambled eggs onto a platter.

"Oh, I think I need to clean up first. I held that squirming calf on my lap for the entire ride home."

"Yeah? What's her name?" Kate inquired. "If an animal lives on this farm, we always name it."

Megan poured a cup of coffee and contemplated Kate's question. "You know, I think we'll let Felicity and Luke name her. I'm fresh out of ideas. And I'm also fresh out of suitable clothes. I don't know what my mother was thinking when she packed a bag for me. I'm more prepared for a tropical vacation, not for any kind of serious work here. Can I get a ride into town this morning?"

Kate nodded without looking up. "Sure, I'll take you whenever you're ready."

Megan climbed the steps one at a time. She didn't know that so much could happen between dawn and breakfast, but now she'd experienced first hand that it was long enough to save even the smallest of lives.

She wasn't proud of the way she'd acted when they were at the Prescott ranch. It wasn't like her to be so aggressive and hostile and maybe even a tiny bit vindictive. It was a stupid fight, considering Bristol Bay Farms had plenty of pasture land and the grazing cattle didn't hurt anything. It was more about the way those cowboys had sabotaged the fences that got Megan riled. But then, she secretly enjoyed the adrenaline rush of the fight, especially the look on Nolan's face when he realized he'd been outmaneuvered. She momentarily considered calling him and rubbing it in his face, hoping to start another fight with him.

This was entirely new to her. Megan had been brought up saying, *Yes ma'am* and *Yes sir*, no matter what she actually thought, making the transition to, *Yes, Chef*, even easier. Then, after her marriage, it progressed to, *Yes, Steve*. The thought of talking back or disagreeing never occurred to her until now. And it felt good, wielding her power to save that calf. But it was a one-time thing, even though thinking about it again gave her another rush.

A hot shower and clean clothes went a long way in fixing her mood. She was closing the doors to her bedroom balcony when she was distracted by a noise.

Romeo was back. Only this time he was less of a bull and more of a bully. And possibly a bit more dangerous.

"What are you doing here?" she demanded.

Nolan tipped his hat back on his head a little and smiled up at her. "Why don't I come up there and we can talk about it?"

Megan had a thought that maybe she had somehow summoned him here by reliving their argument. But now it seemed that he was inviting himself to her bedroom. And she was considering it, which meant that she was out of her ever-loving mind.

She leaned over the balcony and called down to him, "No, I'm afraid I'm too much of a mess to even consider having company. How about you just tell me why you're here?"

Nolan laughed and smiled at her convincingly. "No, ma'am, I think you've misunderstood my intentions. I only came here to keep you updated on your new calf, Elsa."

"You named her Elsa?" Megan inquired.

"No, your man in the barn named her. The vet called me and told me about your predicament. Since it's healthier to feed the calf colostrum from the mother than it is to feed her replacement colostrum, I decided to bring it over."

"And how did you do that? I didn't know you were dairy farmers," Megan dryly noted.

"Well, we might not be dairy farmers but cows are the same no matter what business you're in. And the milk always comes out the same way. It might be a little harder for us because we had to manually do it but if you wanted to buy us a milking machine, we could get milk for her every day."

"Do you mean that you'd have to bring the calf some milk every day? I imagine it would be almost impossible to do that. How about we buy that cow and save everyone the inconvenience? It can't be easy for you, taking out time to come over here. I remember you saying that calf wasn't worth saving. So why are you really here?"

Nolan squinted in the sun. He'd underestimated Megan and now he might not ever find another reason to come and visit her every day. He had to go all in. "Sorry, can't sell her but I'd consider leasing her to you."

It wasn't as good as owning the cow but it was better than the alternative. "Sure. Talk to Luke on your way out." She momentarily thought about apologizing for her behavior that morning but then realized it would only make her look weak. It was bad enough that she'd gone there looking like she'd forgotten to wear pants. She abruptly ended their conversion with a cheerful, "See ya," before closing the balcony doors and retreating into her room.

Megan had to sit down for a few minutes to calm her racing heart. She couldn't tell if he was trying to irritate her on purpose or if he was simply an irritating person. Whatever it was, she was going to make a point of avoiding him from now on. Once the cow was in the barn with her calf, she could go back to whatever she'd been doing before she met him. It was just that, at this very minute, she was having a hard time remembering exactly what that was. But she was sure, like her racing heart, her temporary amnesia would eventually pass. She grabbed her purse and went downstairs to find Kate waiting by the front door. One look at Kate's face and Megan knew her secret was out.

"You heard?" Megan asked while inwardly cringing.

"Everyone heard. We couldn't help it, with all that hollering," she admitted. "I'm guessing that he's not your type unless that's the impression you were hoping to give him. Because it was very effective. You almost had me convinced."

"Honestly, Kate, I'm just hoping to make it through the day. He's not high on my list of things to do."

Kate nodded knowingly. "Well, I have a feeling your list will change. The nights get long and lonely out here on the farm. And when you're alone long enough, even a handsome, lanky legged cowboy like him might appeal to you. And he looks like the type that could keep you busy."

"Well, I'm busy enough right now and I'm not going to worry about the nights. I sleep just fine," Megan told her.

Kate laughed. "I wasn't talking about sleeping. It seems like you've made up your mind but be ready to change it. Those Prescott men are hard to resist. I'll give you two months before you start to see things differently. Even if your heart is on vacation now, seeing him will heat up your blood pretty quick."

Megan did her best to look shocked. "I never said he was unfortunate looking. I just said that he wasn't exactly what I'd be looking for. If I was looking, which I'm definitely not."

"Maybe, but you might want to give it some time before you scare him off. There's not much to do out here. That's why I keep a place in town."

"Really? Do you have roommates?" Megan asked.

"Something like that. We should go before the stores get busy," Kate volunteered. "Clothes shopping can be hard and I have a feeling this is going to take the whole day."

Megan chuckled to herself. She was going to enjoy seeing the surprised look on Kate's face when they were finished in less than an hour.

WHEN MEGAN ASKED for a volunteer to help Luke, Felicity didn't notice that everyone was looking at her. It never occurred to her that anyone else had noticed how she felt about Luke. She'd been hiding her feelings for so long now that it was just second nature for her.

Just because she was hiding her feelings didn't mean that she wasn't still hoping he would notice her. She stopped in her bedroom before she left to put on some lip gloss, shorten the straps on her bra and unbutton the top two buttons of her shirt. He was still a man, after all. Then she hurried to the barn to see Luke.

The barn looked empty, except for the calf curled up on a tarp next to one of the stalls. Luke came around from the other side, carrying a big bale of hay. His strong shoulders, his green eyes... Felicity had to take a deep breath and focus on the calf.

"I guess you named her Elsa?" Felicity smiled and moved closer to Luke. She watched as he opened the bale and spread a thick bed of hay for the calf.

Luke stood up and brushed off his hands. "What do you think of her? She's a little one but very inquisitive. You can pet her if you want."

Felicity knelt to touch the calf's soft nose. "She's adorable and so lucky you brought her back with you. What happens to her now?"

"The vet is bringing some splints for her front legs but right now I have to rig up some kind of a sling for her so she can eat when her mama gets here."

"Do you need help? I know how to sew," she offered. Even as she said them, the words sounded awkward to her.

Luke grinned at her. "It's not that kind of a project but I'll keep you in mind if I ever need something sewn. I've already cut a strip of tarp and just need to find a way to hold Elsa at the right height but I won't know what that is until her mama gets here."

Felicity casually put her hands on her hips, hoping Luke would notice that she'd developed an attractive figure. But then, she'd been hoping he'd notice her for the last eleven years. She used to be a scrawny twelve-year-old who openly adored him. Now she was a woman who he openly ignored.

"I might be getting an apprenticeship with a local artist," she casually mentioned.

Luke smiled. "Yeah? How'd that happen?"

"He saw my work at the Master's Show in Charlottesville. If he picks me, I'll get to stay around here and have a job."

Luke nodded but didn't look up at her.

She always did this, running out of things to say to him. No matter how often she rehearsed it, everything she said sounded clumsy. The silence between them stretched longer until she remembered his sister, Robin. That might be something to interest him.

"Robin and I are planning to go out some night this week. I know she'd love it if you could come too. She said she doesn't get to see much of you these days."

"Yeah? What's my little sister been up to lately?" Luke asked.

Felicity hesitated to answer, waiting to see if

he'd look at her. She counted slowly to ten and when he was still engrossed with everything but her, she decided to tell him exactly what she was thinking. "That's funny that you still think of her as little. She's the same age as me and we're only three years younger than you."

Luke scowled. "I didn't mean it that way. She'll always be my little sister, even when she has gray hair."

"And I guess I'd know that if I'd had any brothers or sisters. Sorry, Luke," she mumbled.

"No worries. Tell her I'll call her this week and that I'm sorry that I can't make it, what with trying to keep the new calf alive," he told her.

Felicity softly sighed and waved at Luke. "I guess I'll see you later. Let me know if you need help with the calf. Maybe tonight?" she asked hopefully.

Luke nodded. "See you later."

Felicity felt the familiar sting of rejection wash over her like a full-body slap. Someday she might be forced to admit that there wasn't a future with Luke, that it had been a childhood dream. But someday was a long time off. She'd come too far to give up now.

CHAPTER SEVEN

Megan didn't recognize Main Street. Victorian garden lamp posts lined both sides of the street, heavily laden with pink flowers in scrolled metal hanging baskets. It appeared that Main Street had turned into a Norman Rockwell painting. And Kate was right about the traffic. It was barely ten in the morning and the Bristol Bay Fashion Emporium was already crowded.

Kate pointed at a parking spot near the center of the street. "Is this close enough or do you want to circle the block?"

Megan pointed further down the street. "There's a space right in front of the Bristol Bay Feed and Seed supply store. Let's go in there."

Kate answered by gunning the engine and making a fast left into the parking spot. "You sure about this? Intelli-Gwen still owns the store and it's gossip central. She'll tell everyone what size you wear and everything you say so be careful."

"Warning noted, but I think it'll be fun. Coming in with me?" Megan asked.

Kate laughed. "Wouldn't miss it. But remember that I warned you."

Gwen was standing inside the door, ready to greet them the second the bells on the door jingled. "As I live and breathe, I heard you were back. Give me a hug, Megan," said the petite woman while wrapping her arms around her.

"It's wonderful to see you again, Gwen. You haven't aged a day since I was a teenager. How do you do it?" Megan asked with wide eyes.

"Oh, it's simple, honey. I keep busy and never leave the house without putting on my face," she explained with a big smile.

"I don't mean to be nosy, but so many things have changed since the last time I was here. I hardly recognize anything."

Gwen appeared perplexed. "What are you talking about, dear?"

Megan lowered her voice to a whisper. "Well, just looking down this block, Harmon's Market is gone. Did they sell?"

Gwen laughed in relief. "No darling, the town went through a rebranding five years ago. The store's called Bristol Bay Market now."

"Oh, now I get it. The hardware store and the pharmacy too. It must make everything easy to remember."

Gwen raised a finger and nodded. "Did you hear about Janice Portway's daughter, Deloris? The one who used to live in Richmond?"

Megan shook her head. "No, but then I've been gone for a while."

Gwen leaned closer to her. "You didn't hear this from me but I guess she's doing strange things. Bags her trash and takes it directly to the dump."

Megan nodded approvingly. "That's nice. I like knowing that this town is taking recycling seriously. Going green and all that."

Gwen squinted. "Sure, everyone's been doing that for ages but that's not what's going on with Deloris. She's convinced that the CIA is stealing her trash and that aliens will fry her brain with microwaves if she stops wearing that helmet made out of tin foil. Janice says it's because she's off her meds but most people think Deloris joined one of those conspiracy cults."

Megan looked to Kate, hoping for support but Kate just rolled her eyes and shrugged. "Speaking about conspiracies, I just remembered that I'm out of nail polish remover. I'll be over at Bristol Bay Medicine Shoppe."

As soon as the door closed behind Kate,

Megan took a step closer to Gwen. "So Gwen, I need a few things to wear on the farm. Heavy-duty, thick cotton? Imagine a duck blind in the African Serengeti. But you can't tell my mom about any of this. Promise?"

Gwen nodded while picking up a pad and pen. "You've come to the right place, honey. Tell me what you need and I'll get it for you."

Megan smiled, remembering all the reasons why she loved this town. "I need waterproof hiking boots, work boots, cowboy boots and muck boots, size eight. A couple of dozen pairs of lightweight wool socks and boot socks too."

Megan paused to look around the store and saw some wonderful straw hats. "Oh, and an assortment of wide-brimmed hats too. I love that one that looks like something a french sailor would wear."

"You know what you can't live without, dear?" Gwen hinted. "Gaiters. You really can't do without them."

"Really? Well then, I guess I should get two. I don't know where I'll put them but it sounds like an adventure," Megan mused.

"Anything else?" Gwen asked while motioning toward the sportswear section.

"Yes, cotton pants. And do you have those long sleeve cotton shirts with the collars and the little pockets on the front? You know, with pointed flaps and a button? I think they're so cute."

Gwen's head bobbed while she took notes. "Sure, sure. What color?"

"Ahh, khaki, and that brush green. Maybe light brown. Oh, jeans too. Straight leg and boot cut. That should get me started."

Gwen put down her pad and came at Megan with a measuring tape. She mumbled numbers under her breath and then set out pulling stock from the shelves. When the piles were sorted and bagged, Gwen helped carry them to her red jeep with *Bristol Bay Farms* written on the side. It appeared that the rebranding extended into the country too.

"Thanks, Gwen. You're a lifesaver but I'm sure you already know that," Megan told Gwen while hugging her. "Now, I have to try and find Kate because she has the keys to the jeep."

Gwen shook her head and pointed to the keys hanging from the ignition. "You're not in the big city anymore. No one's locked anything in this town for two hundred years. Now you just go on and have a wonderful day, honey!"

Megan started the jeep and edged it down the street until she could park directly in front of the drug store. It occurred to her that Kate probably had loads of work to do but still offered to bring her to town anyway. All of her cousins had been more than welcoming, something that she didn't deserve. Every time that Megan started to feel guilty because she hadn't seen her family in so many years, she resolved to strengthen her relationships with them. Especially with her cousins.

While searching through the aisles looking for Kate, Megan saw a good friend of hers who had been the head chef at the restaurant that just closed. "Hey, James! I didn't know you lived here. How have you been?"

The big burly man was known for his loud laugh and exquisite taste in food. But what she saw on his face now wasn't the man that she remembered.

"Oh, Hi, Megan. Just picking up a prescription for Marcy."

"Yeah? Is she okay?"

"The doctor said it's strep throat so it's just some antibiotics. He said she'd be fine in a few days."

"What is she now, nine? How's Diane?"

"She's good. We've been living with her parents. Diane wanted to move back home so I've been looking for a job around here. I'm still optimistic. It's only been a few weeks and I'm sure I'm going to find a job soon."

"That's great. I'm sure you will too because you're an excellent chef. I really miss your lemon mousse truffles," Megan said wistfully.

When James picked up his prescription and tried to smile, Megan noted how much he'd changed in the weeks since she'd last seen him. Being a chef wasn't glamorous. They'd worked long hours in a hot smelly kitchen, making slightly over minimum wage. Most nights everyone in the kitchen went home exhausted and sweaty. She didn't miss it.

"How about you? Are you having any luck?" he asked hopefully.

"No, I'm not even looking. I never had your talent, James. I was just someone who could make a tomato look pretty. I'll keep you in mind if I hear about any jobs," Megan reassured him before she left.

Megan found Kate in the magazine aisle, her head buried in a gossip magazine. She snuck up behind her and started reading over her shoulder.

"So this is why you ran out away from Gwen? To come here and read about gossip?" Megan teased her.

Kate jumped and faced Megan with her mouth open. "Don't you know how impolite that is? You'd be so embarrassed if I was reading a dirty magazine instead of this bland recounting of a movie star's Tinder account."

"Haha, really funny," Megan deadpanned. "Now you're the one who's going to be embarrassed because all the dirty magazines are kept behind the counter. And I know that because I asked. But I was too young at the time and they wouldn't let me buy one. So, are you ready to go? I drove the jeep around to the front of the store."

Kate glanced up sharply. "You're seriously ready to go? That's a world record, getting out of there in one piece in less than an hour."

"I told you it wouldn't take very long. Sometimes, I'm good at making up my mind and when it comes to clothes, I get in and get out as fast as I can."

Kate looked doubtful. "What could you have possibly bought in that feed store?"

"First, it's called Bristol Bay Feed and Seed, and second, try to imagine what kind of clothes you'd wear if you'd gone on a safari sixty years ago. Think Meryl Streep and Robert Redford in Africa. That will give you a general theme of my new wardrobe," Megan told her while trying to keep a straight face.

Kate laughed, covering her mouth to stifle the noise. "You have to be kidding. You didn't. Please say you're kidding because I don't want to be in the room when Aunt Alice finds out."

Megan nodded. "My mom's gonna have a fit when she sees that every inch of my body is covered with stiff water repellent tan cotton."

They both laughed until other customers frowned at them. Megan pulled Kate aside and confided in her. "Kate? I've been meaning to ask you this, but since I've been gone so long and you were what, just sixteen when I left? I don't feel like we ever knew each other back then. But now that we're together and we're cousins, I feel like we should be closer and I'd like it if you were less formal with me and I'll try to be more open with you. It's hard for me sometimes and especially now. All of you are so close to each other and I'm an outsider, an interloper in your lives."

Kate squirmed and gave Megan a hesitant look. The silence between them dragged on a few seconds too long before Megan realized the explanation for her behavior.

"Oh, I'm so sorry, Kate. I thought it was okay for me to approach you with this but you're obviously not comfortable with talking about it and I don't blame you. I haven't been around and you don't know me so there's no reason for me to think that you'd want to be my friend. I promise I won't ever bring it up again. I'll be outside when you're ready to go."

Kate grabbed Megan's arm as she turned to leave, a horrified look on her face. "No, that wasn't what I was thinking at all. I was thinking just the opposite, that I would love to have you as my cousin and for us to be friends but…"

Megan looked at her curiously. "But what? Is something wrong?"

Kate looked at her feet and slowly nodded. "It's just that your mom asked us to take care of you and to make sure that, you know, you were doing okay and that you liked it here," Kate awkwardly told her.

"Wait. Did she ask you or tell you, as in command you? That's alright. You don't need to answer me because I'm pretty sure it was more of a threat than a suggestion," Megan fumed.

She hadn't seen this one coming. Her beautiful mother with her perfect hair and manners had gone behind her back, sabotaging her relationship with her cousins, all in the hope that she would stay there.

Her mother didn't trust that her daughter could follow through with anything, which wasn't entirely her fault. It was possible that she still saw Megan as a teenager who would do anything to get out from underneath her mother's ever-watchful eye.

"Listen Kate. I'm sorry about what my mom said or if she threatened you because we both know that she's entirely capable of leveling subtle threats. But I can tell you one thing for sure. She can't fire you and she doesn't have any say over who stays and who goes. That's something we would decide together as a family and we would always be there to help each other."

Somehow, Alice's overwhelming desire to keep

Megan happy had alienated everyone around her, made them feel uncomfortable and unsafe, and worried about their jobs. Megan's first impulse was to talk to Alice about it until she realized that Alice would tell her things like how she loved her and wanted to be happy because the most important thing in her life was to have happy children. It would last for hours and they'd both end up crying with Megan apologizing.

"I wish we could start over and you could see me as your cousin and a friend and someone who wants to get to know you because I already think the world of you. I think you're talented and exuberant and beautiful. And sweet Felicity. Is all of this with my mom somehow tied up with her too? Because Felicity always looks so uncomfortable when she's around me or is that just what she's normally like?"

Kate looked at her hands and remained quiet. "There's not anything I can tell you about other than it has nothing to do with you, Megan. But it might have something to do with that tall, good-looking, golden-haired boy in the barn."

Megan's mouth fell open. "Really? I can't believe that I didn't pick up on that! It explains so much. How long have they been dating?"

Kate scoffed. "It's been going on since she was about twelve years old. Her best friend from school is Luke's little sister, Robin. I think she officially fell in love with him when she was about fifteen, but he doesn't know and Robin doesn't know either, and that's the way she wants it to stay. I think she would literally die if he found out."

Megan stared at her in shock. "But Felicity is so beautiful...and polite...and quiet. Oh, I get it. She's just a little too polite, is that what you're saying?"

Kate quietly shook her head. "That's not even half of it."

"I wish there was some way to push it along. Maybe give him a subtle hint that she's interested in him?" Megan asked.

Kate sighed. "We've tried all the normal things without being obvious but he just doesn't see her. She'll always be his sister's little friend and that's all."

"I don't know about that, but I do know a little about men," Megan wryly noted. "And I know that it takes very little to turn their heads. Is he dating somebody right now, somebody he's interested in?"

Kate laughed. "They both seem to have the same personality. Luke doesn't know he's good looking and he doesn't get the hint when women try to flirt with him. He doesn't seem to understand that there are so many girls he could be dating right now. He's just Luke. He lives in the tack room, he's always available, a perfect employee, smart, talented. He's got a heart of gold but for some reason, he's not the type of guy who's comfortable hitting on a random girl."

Megan raised an eyebrow. "I bet we can help them. Just a little, of course. Are you in?"

"I'll brush up on all the classic Rom-Coms," Kate offered. "My favorite movie is the one about a wedding."

Megan smiled. "They're *all* about a wedding."

CHAPTER EIGHT

Megan wasn't exactly nostalgic, but she did like to have a few simple luxuries. One of those luxuries was having enough room to display her pictures and other precious keepsakes that she'd collected over the years. Now that she had a real home, she could finally get out those mementos, knowing that she'd never move them again. So it was a special day for her when she went to her storage locker to pick out some boxes to bring back to Cove House.

The items in her storage locker consisted of personal things: her favorite books, framed pictures, and a small collection of antique perfume bottles. She hadn't saved anything that would remind her of Steve, not that he'd ever given her anything that would remotely qualify as sentimental. Steve was more the practical type, a numbers man you might say, with a less than romantic side to him when it came to Megan. He always seemed to give his mother and sisters jewelry or expensive pieces of crystal. Megan never knew if he'd picked out those gifts by himself or if his secretary had bought those things for him. He'd never asked Megan to do it even though she thought she was pretty good at selecting out gifts.

When she left the little starter house in Virginia Beach, the only thing she saw in her future was a passport, so she hadn't saved the normal things like furniture, dishes, lamps, or any other of the practical things you need when living in a house. At one point she offered Steve the bulk of the contents of their home, but he refused on the basis that his new apartment was too small. So, in the end, a truck from the local charity shop was the lucky recipient of sixteen years of her life. It felt oddly freeing to let go of things she no longer loved from a life she no longer had.

It's funny how she remembered things differently than the way they actually happened. She remembered packing for days, carefully wrapping everything in layers of paper and meticulously taping the boxes closed. But the first thing she thought when she lifted the rolling door to her locker was that it looked empty to her. The boxes were neatly stacked around the outside of the storage locker, leaving plenty of room for her to look at labels and pick the boxes that she wanted.

But as she went through what was there, it occurred to her that she didn't have enough to warrant storing them for the next fifty years. It made much more sense to bring her scattering of cardboard boxes back to Cove House. So she backed the jeep right to the entrance of her locker and started loading. Except for the boxes with books, the rest were lightweight and she easily moved them, piling them in the back and only stopping at the rental business office long enough to pay her bill and cancel her rental.

There was one box that stood out from the rest. Mainly because the contents shifted inside the box when she placed it in the jeep. Megan didn't remember packing that box and it looked more like something Steve would use, so when she got back to the jeep she pulled off the top and looked inside. The box was filled with accounting papers, tax returns, accounting sheets, and all those boring things that Megan had never felt curious about.

She looked through a few more papers before noticing that there were duplicates of a lot of things. And then she wondered why Steve would have their personal papers and his business papers at home. He usually kept those types of documents in a locked filing cabinet instead of throwing them into an unmarked box.

Her stomach sank and she uttered an audible, "Nooo…" when she realized that she was going to have to contact Steve and find out if this was something that he needed. It was basically her worst nightmare.

In the middle of her inner screaming and emotional shakes, she realized that she still had the mover's phone number and all she had to do was call and get the address where they'd delivered Steve's belongings. And so, with clammy hands, she called and entered his address into her phone for driving directions.

It turned out that Steve wasn't living in an apartment after all. The address seemed to suggest he was living in a house.

Well, good for him, Megan thought. Maybe he was finally able to get a place that's big enough to put a barbecue grill in the backyard and he could stop talking about how much fun it would be to sit outside and cook dinner.

She drove to a suburb of Virginia Beach and then slowed when she got to his street, checking all the house numbers until she found it. The movers had been mistaken because this wasn't an apartment or a starter house either. It was a grand traditional mansion sitting right on the Chesapeake Bay. Megan chuckled a little, wondering if Steve also was forced to come here to retrieve his boxes.

But the more she tried to explain away the discrepancy between what Steve said and what was visible to her now, the more her curiosity got the best of her. In the end, she conducted an online county record search for the address. When the results popped up that Steve Richards had purchased this house two years ago, Megan was stunned.

Two years ago, he told her they couldn't afford to buy a house or a car. Two years ago, she was working seventy hours a week to help pay the bills. They'd never taken a vacation or bought a piece of furniture that wasn't used. Two years ago, they were still happily married. Maybe they weren't falling into each other's arms every twelve seconds, but they were actively pursuing life, love, and happiness.

Her movements became robotic as she got out of the jeep and walked through the gate and up the long stone driveway to the front door. Through the expansive windows, she could see an open, two-story, grand foyer, and a curved staircase covered in turquoise carpet, pieced to make waves with bright yellow and navy blue inserts. *Odd choice to bring Southern Florida into a traditional style house,* she thought. Steve would never do something so gaudy. Now she was certain that all of this was a horrible mistake and she was at the wrong house.

The sunlight reflected off of something metal inside and it momentarily blinded her. Curious, she moved closer to the windows to get a better look at it. And then, she saw what appeared to be a golden statue of Poseidon, standing just over eleven feet high, wielding his trident and asserting his authority over the sea.

It couldn't be described as anything other than a charmless monstrosity. Megan likened it to finding an elephant in the produce aisle of a neighborhood market. The absurdness of it would keep anyone openly and shamelessly staring.

She rang the doorbell, certain that everything could be cleared up in a matter of minutes. A young woman promptly opened the door a crack and peered back at Megan, her black silky hair flying through the opening.

Megan smiled at her. "I think I'm at the wrong house but could you help me anyway? Do you happen to know if Steve Richards lives around here?"

The girl looked uncertain but opened the door all the way, showing her very pregnant belly and a large diamond on her left hand. They stared at each other, neither of them talking. They didn't have to.

Megan's words were filled with pain. "When's the baby due?"

The girl looked down and circled her belly

once before replying. "Three weeks."

Megan looked into her eyes. "Married?"

The girl hesitated before replying. "Soon. Probably right after the baby's born."

Megan's mind went blank as she nodded and turned to walk back down the long driveway. She felt drugged, each second spanning a lifetime of memories. She had flashbacks of struggling through endless doctor visits, countless sticks from needles, painful injections, pills, pregnancy tests, headaches, bloating the persistent pain and unfathomable fear that this month was not going to be *the* month.

She'd done all of that and more for Steve and somewhere along the way, she lost her optimism, spiraling into a fatal orbit that ultimately landed her here. Right smack in the middle of his driveway; an unwilling witness to his abominable infidelity.

It appeared that Steve had found a new life long before they even talked about divorce. But the fact that he'd found another girl who was a teenager turned him into some sort of a legal pedophile in her mind. She finally understood the odd looks she got from strangers when she was that age, kissing a man who was old enough to be her father.

It seemed like a paradox, that a man who thought only of himself would so desperately want offspring. He never wanted anything that implied a commitment, even something as small as a goldfish, because he didn't have time for things like that. Just like he didn't have time for football games or going to the ballet or even walking two blocks to watch the Macy's Thanksgiving Day Parade. All those years they'd lived in New York City and he never once joined her on visits to the Guggenheim or the Museum of Modern Art.

She'd applauded him for his work ethic and his ability to focus on their financial future instead of his immediate happiness. Planning for the future, my ass. He was probably on the internet, searching for any girls who had turned eighteen that day.

Megan realized that Steve was also a soulless gutless coward who used her as a shield, blaming her any time his parents were disappointed in him. Poor Steve, the martyr, married to a barren woman with a stupid job who had no talent. It was no wonder she felt worthless by the end of their marriage. It was no wonder she didn't get her own lawyer. She had gradually turned into the spineless embodiment of all Dorothy's friends; she was brainless, heartless, and a coward.

Megan looked up and realized she'd driven back to Cove House without seeing a single car, a single stoplight, a single anything. The only thing she could see was the burning flames of rage.

She rested her head on the steering wheel and closed her eyes. Maybe the earth would swallow her up or one of those planes that are always dropping from the sky would land on her jeep and she could leave at the same time as all of her memories stored in those boxes. It would be like she'd never even walked the planet.

There was a knocking on her window and she turned her head slightly to see Luke smiling at her. "Do you need help carrying your boxes inside?"

Megan didn't answer and turned her head until her forehead was pressing down against the steering wheel again. She could hear Luke emptying the jeep and then it got quiet.

A few minutes later he was back, knocking on her window. "Sorry to bother you but Felicity and I need you to come out to the barn. Do you have time right now?"

It looked like Megan wasn't not going to have the time right now to explode in the flames of a plane crash. She'd have to put it on her list for tomorrow.

"Sure," she told him. "I'll be there in two seconds." It was enough to get him to leave her alone for a few more minutes.

She decided that she couldn't decide anything, that the only thing she was sure about was that she could never again be sure about anything. She'd listened to Steve's lies and never for a single moment suspected that he was lying to her. Was she that stupid or was he that good at lying? Did he really have business trips or was he having romantic interludes with other women?

The more she thought about it, the more she felt herself spiraling into despair. And she wasn't going to let him take another day, another minute of her life from her. She made a vow to never let a man manipulate and discredit her again. And for now, all she could hope for was that someday all of this would be a distant memory.

CHAPTER NINE

Nolan had started later than usual today, searching along the streams and creeks that ran through his neighbor's property. His grandfather told him that the old homestead had been located close to water, maybe a river or a large stream. But that's all there was on this land; it was flush with more water than any land he'd ever seen. So after he ruled out the larger rivers, he started riding deeper into the trees and undergrowth, checking for that monolith rock.

His horse stopped short and snorted, pricking his ears forward and straining his head to the right. This was never a good sign and meant his horse had heard something unexpected, something that made him nervous. Nolan dismounted and pulled out his rifle, looking to the side where his horse was watching. He thought he heard the faint sound of a woman crying, although sometimes animals could mimic that sound. When he followed the sound deeper into the wooded area, it led him to a peculiar sight. That beautiful neighbor was lying face down against a boulder with her arms out on both sides, sobbing softly.

Lots of things went through his head. Why is she out here all alone? Why does it look like she's sleeping on that boulder? Why is she crying? She had more clothes on today but the image of her from the first time he saw her was still there, haunting his thoughts.

Nolan cleared his throat, hoping it would announce his presence. But she continued to sob. So he tried using her name. "Megan? Is that you?"

Megan tried to lift her head but it fell back to the rock, something that could only mean she was in trouble. Real trouble. He dropped his rifle and climbed to where she was trapped. "I'm going to get you out of there," he told her. "It looks like your foot's caught. Does it hurt?"

"Yes, it hurts. It feels like a million tons of rock is crushing it. I was climbing up this rock and slipped and now my left foot is wedged. I tried to take off my shoe but I couldn't reach it and If I try to stand and put weight on that leg, the pain is unbearable. All I can do is lie here and cry," she told him between sobs.

"Don't you have a phone?" Nolan asked her

while using his hunting knife to dig around her foot. "It's dangerous to come out here by yourself, especially this close to nightfall. Seems to me, you were on a suicide mission."

"I'm not going to argue with you," she sniffled. "So if that's what you're after, you can just leave now. I'll stay here and wait for all the raccoons and coyotes to come and eat me. Don't worry, I saw my fate and accepted it hours ago. I'll be fine."

Nolan was too worried about her foot to argue with her. "It looks like your foot's twisted. It might be a sprained ankle or something worse so when I get it freed, you might have more pain. Try not to scream. I left my horse untied and the last thing we need is to lose him right now. Are you ready?"

Nolan didn't wait for an answer. He sliced through the sides of her hiking boot and then cut the laces. Once he was sure that her foot had enough room to come out of the boot, he buried his knife in the crack he'd made and used it as leverage, opening it long enough to pull her foot out of the boot.

"Don't move your left foot or try to step down," he gently told her. "Feel around with your right foot and once you're steady, just lean into me and let me catch you."

Nolan was surprised at her endurance for pain. She hadn't made a sound but her ankle and foot were blue and already starting to swell. There wasn't any way for him to know how long she'd been out here or why none of her people had come looking for her. But he was sure that a woman like her certainly had to have a man or someone that cared for her. And then he realized that he cared about her. Not in the way you'd want to help anyone who was hurt, but in a possessive protective way, like she already belonged to him.

"Dammit, I just wish..."

"What do you wish?" Megan asked.

"I wish you had someone to tell you when you couldn't do things like this. You never should have been out here alone. Once you get out here in the woods, there's no sense of direction. You're not a homing pigeon with a built-in navigation system, Megan. I can't even begin to tell you what could have happened to you."

"And you think this could all have been avoided if I had a man to tell me what to do?" she retorted.

"Yes. Maybe. But I know for sure that we don't have time to fight about this right now. We need to concentrate on how we can get you home in one piece. We're closer to the ranch so if I can get you up on my horse, maybe we can both ride. But it'll be hard to do since you can't put weight on your left foot. And look, now the sun's going down. This is just great," he huffed.

MEGAN HAD WOKEN up this morning still reeling from yesterday's discoveries. It felt like a bad dream, something you shudder when you remember and then quickly put it out of your mind. It would have been easier if their entire marriage had been filled with a long list of his infidelities. But then, there was a good chance this wasn't Steve's first. It was just the first time he'd been caught.

She'd slept in after a late-night binge of wine and movies. Not the kind of movies that have a plot but the kind that has a history. When she was checking all of the closets for some kind of a gun or rifle, she'd found a stack of home movies in her grandma's hall closet. The cans of film were sitting right next to the projector, basically inviting her to watch them. After she'd lugged the projector and movies up to her bedroom, she only came back downstairs long enough to get a bottle of wine. Then she locked her door and sat back, ready to be entertained by the strange antics of people who could be seen and not heard.

If that was the extent of her reaction to finding a pregnant woman in a house that she didn't know Steve could even afford, her cheating husband and his child girlfriend were lucky. Most women would have gone over there and tried to burn down the house with them still in it. But then, most women wouldn't have graciously left a marriage of sixteen years without a fight.

Megan's decision to take a late afternoon walk had nothing to do with the rage she still felt every time she thought about Steve. It was more to do with the nasty hangover that was beating a steel pipe against her skull.

She'd done the responsible thing and left a note, telling Luke and Felicity where she was going. But she'd set down her phone on the kitchen counter when she'd written the note and then forgotten to pick it back up.

The only problem with taking a walk in the woods was that the tree canopy blocked the sun and since her sense of direction was already less than accurate, it wasn't long before she was utterly and completely lost.

She tried breaking sticks, dropping stones, anything that she could remember that might help her. She regretted not taking a wilderness training course when she was in Girl Scouts. She regretted leaving her phone behind. And then she found the highest rock and climbed it, hoping to see some landmark that she remembered. That's when she slipped.

Was it fate that brought Nolan to her? Because if he hadn't been there, she most certainly would've died. And maybe that's what a tiny part of her wanted. But when she saw his face and realized she's been saved, she found that she might have a reason to live after all.

Now, there are all those things that people say about men. That the best way to get over a man is to find a new man. And maybe she wanted to get back at Steve. But it was more that she needed a man to look at her, really look at her like she was desirable.

Whatever it was that she needed, she felt like Nolan was the man to give it to her. She was flat on her back on his sofa with her freshly bandaged foot propped high on pillows. And she was feeling great, thanks to taking a handful of the pain medicine that the Doc left behind.

Nolan made himself comfortable on the chair next to Megan and took off his hat. His blonde hair was matted so he pulled his fingers through it and turned to her. A slight stubble on his face and his hazel eyes were a complete surprise. For some reason, she thought the three brothers all had dark hair and were as mean as snakes.

"You must be starving. Can I get you something to drink or eat?" he asked her.

Megan nodded. "Yes, all of that and more. I feel like I haven't eaten in days. By chance, do you know how to play the guitar and sing?"

Nolan grinned and shook his head. "No, but I can bring you some wine and some marshmallows to roast in the fireplace if you'd like. But seeing as how you're a grown woman, I didn't think you'd want to make s'mores."

Megan nodded. "That will do, but I'd like it better if you would sing me a song."

Nolan frowned in confusion. "How many of those pain pills did you take?"

"Just a few," Megan semi-truthfully told him. "Do you want to hear something funny?"

"Sure, and then I think we should eat," Nolan told her as he moved to sit on the table in front of the sofa. He leaned toward her until he could feel the heat coming off of her body.

"Well, the morning we met, I couldn't keep all of you straight, probably because of all the confusion and you were all moving around and I had this distinct memory that you had dark hair and eyes."

His eyebrows lifted briefly in surprise. He had no idea that he'd even made an impression on her.

"Are you disappointed?"

Megan looked thoughtful, then shook her head. "No, I don't think so. But I might have been if you were bald."

Nolan stifled a laugh and realized that the pills were acting like a truth serum. Instead of using this to get her to tell him everything she knew about the land on Bristol Bay Farms, he discovered that he was more interested in finding out how she felt about him.

"Really? What do you have against bald men?" he teased her.

"Well, nothing really. I just like your hair. It's kind of thick and wavy and works with the color of your eyes," she told him with a hint of approval.

"Do you want to know what I think about you?" he countered.

Megan rolled her head away from him and stared at the ceiling. "No, I've had enough trauma today already. Maybe some other time, though. Are you completely sure that you can't sing me a song?"

"I have a better idea," Nolan told her. "Why don't you sing me a song?"

"I'd love to but none of my talents revolve around music," Megan explained. "I do better in the kitchen but it turns out I hate to cook."

"Well, you're just a bundle of contradictions, aren't you? I think I should probably change your ice pack now. Doc said you had to keep that elevated and cold but not too cold which means I get to be the one to check it every fifteen minutes. And I need to get you to eat something."

When Nolan started to get up, Megan reached for his hand. "Have you ever known someone who had red hair before?"

Nolan stifled his laugh with a cough. "No, not that I can remember. And not as dark red as yours, anyway."

Megan rolled her eyes. "Thank God. So many people think that just because my hair is red it means I have a short fuse when the truth is I'm actually too patient and understanding. I never get upset about anything. But there is a small chance I'll set fire to your truck if you try to call me Red."

"Is that so?" Nolan bit his lip to keep from smiling. She was charming him, pulling him into a place he'd never been before. He thought about what it would be like to kiss her. She was already lying down with those wide eyes, confessing all her secrets to him. All he had to do was lean closer and maybe she'd kiss him first.

Nolan was jolted back into reality when Megan tried to sit up. "Hey, you can't move your foot like that," he scolded her. "Where are you going?"

"I changed my mind so now you can tell me what you thought when we met. But be kind. I'm kind of fragile right now," she confided while batting her long eyelashes at him.

Nolan's mouth went dry and he wished he'd swallowed some of that truth serum too. Was it a good idea to tell her that his first impression was that she was a little crazy? Crazy in a good sexy way that made him lose focus and that he hadn't stopped thinking about her since then?

He cleared his throat, stalling for more time.

"Well, it's hard to say, what with all the yelling and threats, but I guess, all in all, I was intrigued by you."

Megan sighed. "Was that because you'd never seen a woman in a babydoll nightie in your barn before or because I didn't want you to kill that calf?"

"A little of both to be honest," he admitted.

"Then I'm happy. Now, where's that wine you were talking about?" Megan inquired with a smile.

"Coming right up. You just stay there and I'll be back in a minute," he told her while gently touching her shoulder.

His touch brought back the memory of how it felt to be carried in his arms and how surprised she'd been when he easily lifted her. Megan could get used to all of this attention. She couldn't remember the last time a man had opened a door for her, much less saved her from an evil forest and scurried her to safety on his gallant stallion. And the night was still young. All she had to do was try to stay awake until he came back.

CHAPTER TEN

The early morning quiet was interrupted by squealing brakes and banging on the front door. Megan woke up, her head pounding and her ankle throbbing. She knew who was out there desperately trying to get in. There was only one person who loved her that much. It could only be her mother.

But what Megan didn't know was how Alice found out that she was at the Prescott Ranch. Unless? Of course, it was those rats at Cove House who couldn't keep their mouths shut. Megan was going to make sure they knew she was the boss and ratting on her couldn't happen again. Then she chuckled at how unrealistic that was. When had anything ever stopped her mother?

Her mother swept into the house in a flurry of maternal concern and perfume. "Come on, Megan," her mother ordered her. "We need to take care of that ankle of yours."

Alice Atwood gave Nolan a disapproving glare. She didn't know anything about these men other than they'd kept her daughter all night instead of returning her to Cove House. It was completely unacceptable on principle and also on fact. Megan was injured and incapable of caring for herself. She should have been returned to Felicity so that all of her private needs could be met. Alice couldn't even wrap her head around how they got her daughter to the powder room.

Everyone had worried about Megan when she didn't come home, but they were so relieved when they got the phone call from the Prescotts that they didn't even think to go and get her. It was Kate's day off, so only the younger staff was there. Alice made a mental note to hire more help for the house. If she had known about it last night, she would have been over here, getting her daughter to the hospital for a proper exam and an x-ray. Doc Wilson was a good doctor but he could never replace an x-ray machine.

Megan tried to sit up on the sofa, groaning in pain. "Hi, Mom. Did you meet Nolan?"

Alice stopped wringing her hands long enough to politely smile and shake his hand. "Hello," she managed to say in a kind tone. "Thank you for taking care of Megan. She could have died out there."

Nolan read Alice like he read the Bible. An especially long chapter explaining Southern mothers was included in the Book of Genesis.

"Hello, Ma'am. Glad I could help," he told her with a genuine smile.

Alice took another look at Nolan, narrowing her eyes in the realization that there was something different about Megan and it had everything to do with this man. He had the calm and smile of a man who'd already made his conquest and had taken her daughter's heart.

She was too late to stop that but there was still time to make sure he didn't marry her. She decided right then and there to look into these neighbors. Even though they'd always been inconspicuous and friendly, they were new to the area and hadn't even tried to blend in with the community. They were never at church or helping with any community projects. Sometimes the worst criminals hide in plain sight and she didn't trust anyone when it came to Megan.

"I hope you brought a stretcher, Mom, because I don't think I can put any weight on this ankle," Megan quietly admitted.

Alice nodded while using one finger to press one button on her phone's screen. Seconds later, Luke knocked on the door.

"I brought along help, Megan. I thought you

might not be able to walk yet," her mother curtly informed her.

Alice turned her attention to Luke, who was uncomfortably standing by the front door. "Well, what are you waiting for? You're the one who lost her. Go get her and take her to the car," she ordered.

"Really, Mom?" Megan was appalled by her mother's behavior, just like she'd been as a teenager. Her mother had told her many times that she would understand when she had daughters of her own but the likelihood of that seemed slim. She was just going to have to take her mother's word for it.

"Yes, Megan. As long as you can't walk, I'll be giving the orders. I called ahead to the hospital and they know we're coming."

Megan groaned. "You realize that we'll probably see Doc Wilson there and he's going to wonder why I'm back, begging for more pain pills, don't you?"

Alice's face went pale. "Pain pills? Why on earth would you need pills?" Alice sharply asked. A worried look settled on her face as she examined every inch of the room. She exhaled in relief when she finally spotted the pill bottle sitting on the table.

"Good Lord, Megan, there's nothing that a glass of sweet tea can't fix. I might even put a thimble full of whiskey in it if you're really hurting."

Alice gave Nolan a benevolent look. "Nolan, would you be a dear and throw out those pills? Not down the drain though," she instructed him, "there are already too many drugs in the water."

Alice turned her attention back to Luke, dramatically raising her eyebrows while serving up her best melting look, which, in turn, caused him to give Megan a despairing look.

"Oh, come on Luke. I won't bite you," Megan told him with a wink. The mixed message only confused him more, and he continued to internally debate his decision while his feet remained rooted to the floor.

Nolan knew why Luke was balking. "Fine, I'll do it," he announced as he carefully plucked Megan off of the sofa. "Where do you want her?" And then he smiled at Alice so that she could be certain of his intentions. From now on, no one was touching Megan but him.

LIKE HUNGRY HUMMINGBIRDS, Kate and Felicity had been hovering over Megan for days. The swelling on her ankle was significantly less and she was gingerly walking when she had to. The rest of the time, she waited for Nolan to make his daily visits.

Alice was noticeably angry for exactly forty-eight hours before her attitude suddenly changed. That's when she started bringing Megan sheer peignoirs and encouraged her to wear "a little lipstick" when Nolan was expected to arrive.

Megan was amused by her mother's behavior but not suspicious enough to question her. She knew that her mother thought Nolan had seduced her, but that was because her mother thought all men were tramps and scoundrels. Except for her husband, Walter, of course. The truth was that Nolan had been exceptionally respectful of her in spite of the fact that she was drugged. Or maybe that was the reason for his hands-off approach. The only way she'd know for sure was if she asked him and she was afraid it would sound more like an invitation or accusation than a question.

She played it in her head to see how it sounded; *Excuse me, sir. Why didn't you plunder me when I was too incapacitated to make a decision? Is there something wrong with me or is there something wrong with you?*

The truth was, her heart hadn't properly healed enough to completely trust Nolan and she worried what she would do if time didn't change how she felt. She didn't want to be bitter but she didn't want a man to make a fool out of her again either. She hoped that soon she wouldn't have to choose and her feelings would meld into a more palatable choice.

Megan could tell by the footsteps on the stairs that Nolan was right on time for his noon visit. He spaced them four to six hours apart so he wouldn't miss any sign of her progress. Her forehead suddenly tightened into a knot, realizing why he came to visit her so often.

Was he waiting for her to completely heal before he brought out his seduction moves? Did that also mean that he based his criteria on whether or not she could run first, so no one would blame him for taking advantage of her?

Did you hear about poor Megan? Pity, she couldn't even get up to call for help. Her ankle was irreversibly and fatally sprained, you know.

"Hey, beautiful. How are you feeling?" Nolan leaned over her and for a long second, she thought he was going to kiss her.

Megan contorted her face and whispered, "I'm much worse. I think that now my throat is sprained and it should be on bed rest too. Sorry." An apologetic smile accompanied her explanation.

Nolan looked part confused and part alarmed.

"Do you want me to..."

Megan shook her head.

"Sure, then I'll call..."

Megan shook her head more.

"Do you want me to go?" he asked.

She shrugged and pointed to the door.

Nolan reluctantly stepped away from her. "Call me when you're feeling better, okay?"

Megan nodded and waited until she heard the front door close. And then, just as sure as she was that Nolan wouldn't let the door slam, she was sure that Kate would immediately come up the stairs.

"So what happened?" Kate demanded with both hands on her hips and her head tipped. "What turned his smile upside down?"

"Wow, I wasn't expecting that from you. Aren't you getting tired of him checking on me every four hours? And if he stays an hour every time, that only leaves me with..."

Kate interrupted, waving her hands at Megan. "I get it, really I do. But have you looked at him? I think you need to get your eyes checked because he's the real deal. And he's sweet, Megan. So kind and generous and thoughtful."

"And I think you're desperate to get rid of me," Megan answered dismissively. "Besides, who really knows what the real deal is?"

Kate sighed. "I've never seen two people who are more right for each other and the fact that you brush him off because he cares too much is something I don't understand. You need to get over whatever it is that's keeping the two of you apart, Megan. And do it fast before he goes off and settles for a second-best woman who does want him."

Kate climbed onto the bed next to Megan. "Okay, I'm ready to shut up now. But I'm going to tell you what anyone who loves you would tell you. Don't come crying to me if this love affair never happens because I'm going to say that I told you so. And wag my finger at you while I say it."

"Oh, Kate. Can we talk about something other than a man? Because I have an idea of what we can do with that old tour bus in the barn. We could make it into a traveling food truck and get everyone around here to contribute to it and take turns running it. We could drive it around to restaurants and neighborhoods in town. It would be one-stop shopping for everyone in Bristol Bay with fresh milk and eggs and produce. It would be our very own little side hustle. Doesn't it sound exciting?"

Kate's face lit up. "And there's the Simms Family off Bakersfield Road. They raise alpacas and they have the best yarn and Chelsea has honey and honey butter and honey candles. Plus she has the Cayugas duck eggs. They're hard to find and are the best for baking."

Megan was happy that Kate was excited about the idea too. "And I know an excellent chef who makes to-die-for truffles. He's out of work right now and I know he could sell as many truffles as he can make. What do you think?"

Kate's face became serious. "What about the Prescotts? They sell grass-fed beef and the best beef jerky I've ever had."

Megan whipped around to face Kate. "Which one?" she asked.

Kate played dumb. "What do you mean? Which one of what?"

"Fine, if that's the way you want it I'll go over there right now and interrogate both of them. Which one is it, Blake or Teddy?"

Kate sighed. "It's Blake. Sometimes he comes over during the day. He brings me the beef jerky, that's how I know about it. He's asked me out but my evenings aren't exactly free right now."

"Really? Why not?" Megan asked.

"Oh, it's just something I'm working on. A project," Kate hedged.

"You couldn't be more vague, even if you tried. But I'll mind my own business. What about fish? Does anyone around here have a trout pond? And the dairy with the fresh milk. Do they have fresh butter too? And cream and big blocks of cheese? What about goat's milk? Does anyone have goats? Because in France they have fromage de chèvre, which is wonderful cheese made from goat's milk."

Megan waited for a reply and when she didn't get one, she looked at Kate. Her eyes were closed, her mouth was open, and she was dead asleep. Megan smiled and pulled a blanket from the bottom of the bed and carefully tucked it around

Kate.

Kate had been tired too often lately, making Megan suspect that she was sick or had a boyfriend. Some mornings she came late to Cove House and had to push herself to get everything done. And then there were all of the phone calls. She always kept her phone on silent and would pull her phone out of her pocket, only to hurry off to someplace more private before she answered. Megan knew that everyone had secrets and that she should probably stay out of Kate's business. But a real family intrudes and asks hard questions. It's their job and birthright to meddle.

Right now, the only thing on Megan's mind was getting out to the barn and finding Luke. If anyone could fix up that bus, it was him. But when she tried to put weight on her left ankle, the pain was too much and she knew she'd never make it down the stairs.

She crawled back into bed next to Kate and went back to focusing on her new business. They should take that bus to one of those auto repair places and have the bus painted green, the exact color of grass, and the name of their business should be plastered on all four sides of the bus so everyone could see it, reading "Farm to Fork" in big silver letters. And maybe, they could rivet thousands of bright shiny forks all over the front of the bus, making it look outrageously distinctive, just like the steel spikes on the cars in *Mad Max*.

CHAPTER ELEVEN

Megan's ankle was completely healed. No pain, no bruising, no swelling, and there was no holding her back. She was finally free to do more than sit in her room and think of all the things she could be doing. The very first thing she did was to go out to the barn to see Elsa, the calf. The calf and mother were busy eating and didn't even look up when she came in. Even Luke was busy working on his laptop.

She was curious to see what had him so engrossed. "How's the baby doing out here?" she asked while inching closer to Luke.

Luke looked up and smiled at Megan. "Look at how well Elsa is standing now. She still has splints on her front legs but she's getting stronger and bigger every day."

Megan attributed most of this to the fact that

the calf was united with her mother and getting all the nutrition and love that she needed. As soon as the calf could walk about freely, they planned on putting both of them out to graze in a pasture close to the house.

"When they're put in the pasture, will we put up a camera to watch them? To make sure they're safe?" Megan asked Luke.

Luke was so engrossed in his computer that he didn't look up when he answered. "We'll just send one of the dogs to go out with them."

Megan was confused. She'd never seen dogs on the farm but she always loved dogs and wanted to have one. It's just that her schedule never permitted it before and also there was Steve, the man who didn't want a pet.

"What breed of dog do you use for that?"

Luke hesitated for a few seconds before replying. "It depends on where we're using them. For the cows, probably a Great Pyrenees and maybe we'll put a male llama out there with them to make it completely predator-proof. We don't have a great deal of livestock on the farm, but we do everything in our power to protect them. We have a lot of land out here and that means we have a lot of wild animals roaming around too. Chelsea's ducks and the goats are kept close to Jameson House."

"Goats?" Megan inquired. The only goats she'd

ever seen were on the internet and she thought they were adorable and funny. But they were also noisy and she suspected they'd be harder than Romeo to keep away from the flowers. She wasn't sure if she wanted to wake up to that every morning. Not that she slept in anymore, as it seemed like the longer she was at Cove House, the earlier she woke up. She remembered what Kate had told her about things getting lonely in the country. Luckily, she had more than enough people and projects to distract her.

Megan remembered going to Jameson House when she was little. It was busy there with hordes of workers and giant farm machinery always moving, trucks ripping through the gravel, horn honking and yelling. And that was on a quiet day.

Her mom was right when she said that Cove House was probably the best place for her. She liked the serenity of it. On one side of her room, she had a perfect ocean view, unobstructed by yacht clubs or sailboats tethered to long wooden docks. And she could look out a different window in her bedroom and see endless fields paint-brushed with crimson and gold wildflowers. When she was younger, she used to ride her horse along the river and sit on her favorite rock, making daisy chains and watching smallmouth bass swim around rocky areas and stumps. The endless green pastures and the tranquility of being so close to water are what she really wanted. Cove House was part of Bristol Bay Farms but it felt more like a beach house to her.

"What do you think about the Farm to Fork truck?" she asked Luke. "Do you know how long it's going to take before it's up and ready?"

Megan could tell that this was a project that interested Luke because he finally looked up at her. "Hang on," he told her as he went to his office and brought out a pile of spec sheets to show her.

"Okay, if you look here, you can see that they're going to cut off one side completely and then have it hinged so it flaps down, and then it can be closed back up when we're driving. There's a latch here at the bottom so that when people are ordering, it can't accidentally pop up and hurt anyone.

Oh, I have some bad news. Even though it's a cute idea, the forks that you wanted to rivet onto the front of the truck present a hazard for people and birds. We don't want anyone to accidentally get speared. I know you wanted it because it's whimsical but it's just not practical."

Megan laughed. "You're right. It was just a crazy idea and obviously, this isn't a wasteland. Just the opposite, now that I think about it."

Luke sighed, his face relaxing into a smile, relieved that Megan wasn't upset. He was particularly interested in this project and wanted everything to be perfect.

He continued with his spec sheets. "They're constructing a wall of cabinetry on the inside and we'll have a generator to keep everything cool, a special place for the meat, and a lot of storage space for everything else. While we're traveling, it's important that nothing falls or breaks if we have to stop quickly."

Megan was impressed at how much thought he'd put into this project and appreciative of all his hard work. "That's a great idea, Luke. Which is why I need you. You're probably the smartest person I know and I'm so happy that you want to be part of this."

Luke was embarrassed by the compliment. "Well, this is a project that the cousins are doing. And I'm not a cousin so I understand that my role is just to be on the sidelines."

Megan burst out laughing. "Are you kidding? You're the backbone of this and I wouldn't even have started it if you didn't want to do it. I know that you're not a blood cousin but you're just as important to all of us. You're sharing equally in the profits from this. You knew that didn't you?"

Luke's smile was quick. "Well I don't have very much family and so anything I do here feels like home to me. I love all of you, so yeah, I'm really happy about this. I mean who wouldn't want a little extra money?"

Megan laughed. "No one that I know." She stopped on the way out to pet Elsa. "Has anyone thought of a name for Elsa's mama?"

Luke sighed. "No, I think we resigned to the fact that she's going back in six months. I signed papers for the lease and I'm positive that she'll be going back to Prescott's herd of cattle."

Megan reluctantly nodded. "Well, everyone understands about food being raised and how that works. But since she's already here and we're going to name her, it seems like she's family. I wonder if the Prescotts would consider extending the lease for the rest of her life?"

"I can work on it if you want," Luke suggested. "But I'm pretty sure that you'd have a better chance of swinging that deal than I would."

Megan frowned. "Is that right? What makes you say that?"

Luke massaged his forehead and sighed. "Have you already forgotten that Alice brought me to Prescott's ranch that morning? When she ordered me to pick you up to carry you out to the car, I got a good look at Nolan's face, and there wasn't any way I was going to touch you. That man is big and he looked serious. And you don't cross a man that has that kind of a look on his face when it comes to his claim on a woman."

The words made Megan's heart skip a beat and she felt her cheeks getting warm. "Come on, Luke, you're going to make me blush," Megan warned him.

Luke raised his eyebrows and nodded. "Well, better you blushing than me getting my face smashed in."

Megan dramatically cleared her throat because she needed to change the subject before her whole face turned beet red. "I've been meaning to ask you about the door in my bedroom that leads to the attic. I remember playing in that room when I was a child. Grandma Coreen had it set up as an office and I played on the floor while she worked at a desk. There was one door that was always locked. I asked her why I couldn't go up there and she said it was because no one went up there. In fact, there wasn't even a key."

Luke furrowed his eyebrows. "I'm pretty sure there's a master key for those old locks. Do you want me to look?"

Megan nodded. "Sometimes at night, I think that I hear a noise from up there or it could just be the wind moving the shutters in my bedroom. Is it possible there's a squirrel or an opossum up there? Because if there is, I will seriously lose it if I wake up with any unwanted company in my bed. It was bad enough getting kisses from Romeo."

Luke nodded in agreement. "I'll take a look at that today. Are you going to be here or are you going to be out today?"

"I think I'll go over to the Prescott ranch today and see what Nolan and his brothers are doing. Maybe see about that lease for Elsa's mama," she said, winking at Luke.

The thought of going over to the Prescott Ranch and seeing Nolan made her giddy. Something that had been happening a lot lately whenever she thought about him and she was afraid of what it meant. No man had ever made her feel so nervous.

Megan changed into new clothes, making sure her hair was perfect, and even added some lipstick before she left. She wasn't sure if Kate had a chance to ask Blake about selling their grass-fed beef and beef jerky from the truck, so she was going to use that as an excuse for her visit.

She wondered if Nolan had felt this same level of anxiety when he was coming to visit her multiple times a day while she was on bed rest. He made it seem natural like he'd always been doing it.

She wasn't wired like that, probably because of all the criticism she'd received as a child. There were hard and fast rules in Southern society and she was expected to learn all these lessons as a child so that she would know what was proper and what was forbidden. And showing up uninvited and unannounced was one of the big ones. Just the thought of it made her legs rubbery. But she decided that just this once, she would take a chance. After all, she had a business opportunity and who wouldn't want a new source of revenue?

Megan took another look in the mirror and decided her all tan outfit made her look like a zookeeper so she searched through Grandma Coreen's drawers until she found a brightly colored scarf and tied it to her neck. The pop of color helped a bit but she felt like the scarf was maybe too bright, so she went back to the dresser and put on gold earrings to tone down the scarf. Then she tried to leave the room, only to discover that she wasn't sure about the earrings or the scarf. Then she went back to take them both off.

And then she wondered if she was in love.

MEGAN PARKED THE jeep in front of the house at Prescott Ranch and got out to check around for anyone working outside. She walked toward the barns and realized that the men were all probably busy, riding out to the pastures and checking on the cattle. And since no one had seen her yet, she thought it was best if no one ever knew she'd been there.

She was in the process of returning to the jeep when she heard her name being called. It wasn't Nolan, but his youngest brother, Teddy. Megan was relieved because Teddy had a pleasant personality, unlike the intense Blake.

"Hi Teddy," Megan answered him. "I came over to talk to Nolan but I don't see him around, so tell him I was here and I'll get in touch with him later."

Teddy was concerned by the serious expression on Megan's face. "Is everything okay? You seem worried."

Megan laughed nervously and then realized that she sounded crazy. "No, nothing like that. I just came over to ask him about extending the lease on the cow."

Teddy furrowed his brow. "What are you talking about? Did you just say you're leasing a cow? Like you'd lease a car?"

"Yes. I tried to buy the cow but Nolan said he couldn't sell her. Are you saying now that I could buy her?"

"No. That would be Nolan's decision. I'm a little confused because we've never rented a cow to anyone before and he didn't mention it to me," Teddy admitted.

"Don't all three of you live here together?" Megan asked. "What do you talk about?"

Teddy grinned at her. "We're men. We don't talk about anything. But I heard about the food truck."

Megan laughed. "Let me guess. So, you've heard about the Farm to Fork business and you know we want you to be involved with us, but the three of you haven't discussed it?"

Teddy's face fell. "When you put it like that, it makes us sound..."

"Busy. It makes you sound busy," Megan shrugged. "Sorry for interrupting your day. If you think about it, you can tell Nolan I was here. See you later. Bye Teddy!"

Megan waved, smiled, and ran to her car. Once she was safely inside, she vowed never to do anything like that again. She had a new appreciation for Nolan and his ability to venture out of his comfort zone. Or maybe everything was in his comfort zone. He probably never felt the kind of anxiety that could only be calmed by sitting in a closet with the door closed.

Speaking of closed doors, she needed to get back home for the unlocking of the attic ceremony. She threw the jeep into high gear and peeled away from the Prescott Ranch.

CHAPTER TWELVE

When Megan got home, Luke was already there waiting to open the locked door in her bedroom and was holding a large skeleton key.

"Are you ready to open the door?" he asked. "It's been a long time since anyone's been up there, so you might want to let me go up first. I'll take a broom, do some cleaning and get rid of the cobwebs and then you can come up and look around if you want. I'll check the roof and the windows and make sure that nothing's broken. Because you're right, if we had a raccoon family living up there it wouldn't be long before we had holes in the ceilings."

Megan thought about it for a few seconds and then decided she wanted to see what was up there more than she wanted to worry about critters or spiders or cobwebs.

"How about if you open the door and then we can see if there's a light fixture up there? I don't have anything else to do right now and my curiosity about what's behind this door has plagued me since I was a child."

"Sure," Luke answered. "Just give me a few minutes and I'll call for you."

"I'm going down to the kitchen and see what Kate and Felicity are doing," Megan told him. "Call down for me once you have an idea of what's going on up there, okay?"

While Megan walked down the stairs, she couldn't stop thinking about all the years she'd fantasized about what was in the attic. A magic portal? Antiques? There were just too many options to consider.

Megan smiled when she caught a whiff of something delicious coming from the kitchen. "What's for lunch, Kate? I mean dinner. Sorry. It's going to take a while before I get used to calling lunch by its proper name."

Kate was in the kitchen working on lunch, which everyone called dinner, which was also the main meal of the day. It was never a small meal, but always the best meal.

Kate laughed. "I like it this way because all of the major cooking is done in the morning and after we eat at noon, all I have to do is make sure there's something for everyone to get supper."

Megan leaned over and smelled the spicy soup that was simmering on one of the back burners. "How did you learn to cook like this? I'm beginning to dream about dinner before I even get out of bed in the morning."

Kate put the lid on a pot and got a bottle of cream from the refrigerator. "Before you came, I cooked all of the meals at the Jameson House. If we were planting or harvesting, I could have more than fifty people to feed. Now that I'm here, most days I go home early unless there's something special the next day or there's baking to do."

Megan nodded. "I think everyone's in a good mood when they know you're baking, especially when it's your triple crust apple pie. You do so much for us. I hope you know how much I appreciate it."

Kate laughed. "Felicity does all the hard work around here, keeping everything clean, which isn't exactly my strong area. Dusting always seems like such a repetitive chore, nothing to show for it except for a clean tabletop for twenty minutes."

Megan nodded in agreement. She'd never been very good at dusting or vacuuming but she did it anyway because Steve wanted a clean house. There it is again, Steve. She had to take that word out of her vocabulary because Steve was gone and she never had to see him or talk to him again.

"So Kate, have you had a chance to ask Blake about the Farm to Fork truck?"

Kate nodded without looking up. "He was going to talk to his brothers but I'm pretty sure they want to do it. I know that Blake wants to sell his beef jerky. He has four or five varieties, so I think it will be a fun thing to have on the truck. Do you know when it's going to be up and operational?"

"Not yet, but Luke's working on it. Do you think we need to have a family meeting to discuss who's going to approach the different farms and find out if they want to participate?"

"We've already done that. I think we're more excited about it than you are, even though it was your idea. I've been using the words, side hustle, every chance I've had for the last week," she confidentially told Megan.

"I know what you mean. It's all I've been thinking about from the moment I get up till I go to bed at night and that's what makes me so impatient to get going. I called a friend who was the head chef where I used to work, and he agreed to make truffles. We served a truffle of the day to every single customer at the end of their meal as a complimentary gift."

Kate stared dreamily, her lips fixed in a small smile. "Truffles? I can't remember the last time I had one. I'm probably going to be buying more than I'm selling."

"Don't you think that other restaurant owners would be interested in that? He'd have a steady stream of customers and could depend on selling a certain amount every day. Oh, and he knows someone else who's out of work too. He used to make the best bread, rolls, and croissants for the restaurant. So he's going to be contributing to the truck too," Megan explained.

Kate looked surprised. "Are we going to have enough room on the truck for all of this?"

Megan laughed. "I hope so because if we don't, I'm going to have to barter for another truck."

Felicity stuck her head in the kitchen. "I don't want to interrupt but Luke's calling for you, Megan."

"Oh good. We should all go upstairs and see what's been locked in the attic for my whole life and my mom's whole life. And there's a good chance that Grandma Coreen's never been up there either," Megan excitedly told them.

The door to the attic was open when they reached Megan's room but there was no sign of Luke. Megan carefully stuck her head through the door opening, the light from her room shining on the steep narrow steps.

She saw a light flash and then Luke appeared at the top of the stairs. He had to turn sideways to fit on the staircase and as soon as he was through, he shut the door to the attic.

"This is the craziest thing I've ever seen. The room is completely sealed and there isn't even the tiniest speck of light getting through from the outside. I used my phone flashlight to look around but it's not enough. We're definitely going to need bigger lights," Luke breathlessly told them.

"Slow down, Luke," Megan quietly told him. "You look like you've seen a ghost or something. Think calmly now. There has to be some light. I've seen the attic windows from the ground."

Luke shook his head. "I know. But there's no sign of anything like that up there. The windows must only exist on the outside of the house."

Megan tried to stifle a laugh. "No, that's not possible. Are you sure that you're not imagining all this? Think about it. Why would anyone put a window in at all, then?"

"I guess there are lots of reasons," Luke told her. "To make it look normal, to not arouse suspicion, or maybe to keep something hidden. Those are just the first ones that come to mind."

"To keep what hidden?" Megan asked, nervously biting her lip.

"I don't know what it is. It's a giant crate of some kind and it's the only thing up here. The attic itself is huge with a high ceiling."

Megan looked at the closed door and then turned to Felicity and Kate. "I'm kind of torn right now. Do we leave it alone or get lights and go up there and look around?"

"It's up to you, Megan, but I don't know how looking around could hurt anything. We'll just be looking, right?"

Megan took a breath and exhaled slowly. "Okay, Luke. We'll need the lights and probably extension cords. They'll need to be long enough to reach from this room."

"And new tarps to protect the floor," Luke added. The floor is metal, the walls, and the ceiling too. I'm guessing it's made from sheets of stainless steel welded together to form one cohesive shell."

Megan perked up. "A shell? Like the shell of a ship? This is all so exciting."

"Maybe we can use the handheld spotlights before we roll out all the heavy-duty stuff?" Felicity asked, looking to the others for support.

Kate popped up and bolted for the kitchen. "I'll be right back! Don't you dare go up there without me," she called to them.

When she returned, they all turned on their headlamps and lanterns Kate brought from the kitchen and went single file up the stairs behind Luke.

Clearly worried, Felicity called ahead to Luke. "I don't know how you're moving through this without getting stuck. Is it normal for the stairs to be so narrow?"

"No, this is anything but normal. But once you're past the stairs, you'll be in the attic and you'll have enough space, so don't get scared," Luke calmly answered her.

As soon as Megan reached the top of the stairs, she noticed something peculiar. Even though it was a hot summer day, the room was eerily cool and dry. Attics usually smell musty, even moldy. This room smelled cleaner than a hospital operating room.

"Wait, guys. Maybe we should go back. I'm getting concerned about all this," Megan whispered. She was feeling uneasy about being up in this room like she was violating something that belonged to someone else. For reasons unknown to her, the attic had been sealed like a tomb.

Luke was already standing by the crate. "There's a shipping label on this but it's in a different language."

Megan stayed by the stairs, watching as Kate and Felicity carefully walked to Luke. The light from their lamps bounced back and forth across the shiny metal room, making an eerie strobe light effect. When they'd made their way to Luke, they were literally standing in the shadow of a large wood crate.

"Where's the label, Luke?" Felicity asked while shining her lamp on the crate.

Luke pointed to the side furthest from them.

"The label's in good condition like it was just put there. But it's not in English. Do you think you'll be able to read it?"

"Won't know until I see it," Felicity answered.

"Oooh," Kate cooed as she flashed her lamp around the room. "The attic is large. Look at how high the ceiling is. And it's nice and cool like it's air-conditioned up here. Isn't that strange for an attic?" she asked.

Luke nodded. "I noticed that too."

Megan was still at the top of the stairs. She'd let everyone walk by her, not because she was afraid, but because she was remembering all the times she'd played in Grandma Coreen's office and had asked about that door. Did her grandma ever come up here and see this room? Did she immediately turn around and go back down the steps, locking the door behind her? Because Megan was having serious doubts about continuing with their quest to find answers.

Luke's forehead furrowed. "The weird thing about the crate is that it had to be constructed up here in the attic, piece by piece. There's no way it could have fit through the door or been pulled up those steep steps."

Megan shook her head in confusion. "But why would anyone do that? Maybe they made the door smaller after the crate was placed up here. Is that possible?"

Luke sighed. "Not likely, although who knows why it ended up here. If you didn't want something that much, why wouldn't you just throw it away?"

Megan stared sadly at the crate. "I think it's the opposite of that, Luke. This was something special, someone cared about the crate and whatever is hidden inside of it. They cared enough to build a steel box around it to make sure it was kept safe from the weather and animals. And maybe they wanted it to be kept safe from us too. Maybe it was too private to ever share with anyone else."

Megan walked closer to the crate, trying to see what was hidden inside it but the wood slats were placed too close together.

Felicity was on the other side of the crate and started reading the address on the label. "It says it's from, Signor Marshall Whitman, Piemonte, Italia, 25 Gennaio 1921 and sent to Miss Emma Sanders, Cove House, Bristol Bay, VA USA. Europeans put the day first and Gennaio means January, so it was sent on January twenty-fifth, 1921."

Luke shot a surprised look at Felicity. "How'd you know that?"

Felicity shrugged. "I like learning languages. It's not a big deal."

"Wait. What happened in Great Grandma

Emma's life during this time?" Megan asked. "Does anyone know where the bible is? The big one that has all of the births, deaths, and marriages recorded?"

Felicity popped her head around the corner of the crate. "It's downstairs in the study. Do you want me to get it?"

"Please," Megan answered gratefully.

When Felicity left to get the bible, Megan walked around the crate so that she could look at the label. "This had to be something that was shipped over the Atlantic, right?"

Luke nodded. "Yes, a steamship. It's at least nine feet tall and six feet wide. You could ship a horse in this."

Megan looked alarmed. "But no one would, right? Please tell me that there's not going to be something dead in there," she asked with a panicked look on her face.

Felicity's head bobbed up the stairs. "What's dead?" she asked.

Kate sighed. "Nothing yet. We're still trying to figure out why this is hidden up here."

Felicity was holding a large bible with gold-edged pages. "Here's the bible, Megan."

"I'm sorry. I can't. Will you look up when Great Grandma Emma got married? Megan begged her. "Her maiden name was Sanders."

"Sure. Wow, this goes back a long time. What

year should I be looking for?" Felicity asked.

"I don't know," Megan impatiently told her. "Just look for Emma Sanders or Emma Jameson. That was her married name and who the Jameson House is named after. It has to be in there."

"Wait. I see it!" Felicity yelled. "She was married the same year that the crate was shipped, on February twenty-first. It was probably a wedding present, don't you think?"

The four of them looked at each other in silence. Luke was the first one to speak. "If it's a wedding present, why is it in the attic? I mean, is there such a thing as an attic present?"

"No," Megan firmly answered him. "It's a Valentine's Day present. The shipping date is towards the end of January and it would have taken about two weeks for this to cross the ocean, so it was supposed to get here in time for Valentine's Day. And this entire room, the way it's lined with steel, is constructed like a ship."

Kate stared at Megan. "How could you possibly know that?"

Megan sighed. "I hate to admit it, but I've watched Titanic half a million times. This attic was lined in stainless steel after the crate was put up here. There's no other way to explain the narrow stairs. Someone went to a lot of trouble to make sure the crate could never leave this room. Almost like they wanted to return it to the ship that brought it, making sure it never reached its destination."

"We're not going to figure this out, standing up here and talking about it," Kate announced. "I'm calling over to Jameson House to have them send Jeff and Howard to help us with this. I don't want it to get all mangled by us trying to open it without the proper tools. If someone took it apart and then put it back together, we should be able to do it too."

Luke studied it from all sides before answering. "That's a good idea. I might need help pulling out whatever's in there." He shook his head, obviously perplexed. "It's a mystery, isn't it?"

Goosebumps crawled up Megan's arms. A mystery in the attic? She felt like she was Nancy Drew.

CHAPTER THIRTEEN

Nolan had always wanted to be a cowboy, something that would seem monotonous to most people. But for him, it was a day that started with a breathtaking sunrise and ended with riding through sprawling pastures, rich in hues of green.

Although it wasn't glamorous, he found a sense of purpose watching the roaming wildlife and working as a part of the unique perfection of life. He wasn't going to give that up, any more than he was willing to give up breathing.

As a child, his grandfather told him stories about growing up in the Maremma region of Italy, moving longhorns, and going on cattle drives. His accounts rivaled those told about the American Wild West and it gave his three grandsons cattle fever.

There was also the family legend of the treasure hidden in Virginia. His grandfather told Nolan the treasure was real but Nolan's father regarded the whole thing as fantasy, something an old man confessed on his deathbed. He'd told his sons that their real power came from staying together, supporting and depending on each other. With the power of three, they could do anything.

Everyone knew the Prescott brothers were a triple threat. They were born with the perfect genetics giving them seductive eyes, voices smooth as butter, and the kind of charm that could only be described as irresistible.

Relying on those gifts had taken them a long way toward fulfilling their ambitions. Someone once told their mother that her sons should have been born with a caution warning on their bottoms. And now, they'd been unleashed on an unsuspecting woman who lived less than a mile away from them.

Lately, only two of those brothers, Blake and Teddy, had been plotting against Megan. They knew the fastest route to getting anywhere was always a straight line, and it seemed that fate had put Megan right smack dab in the center of that straight line. They couldn't believe their good fortune when Nolan rescued her from certain death and brought her back to their ranch house. They stayed behind closed doors the entire night she was there, making sure they didn't interrupt the inevitable. And they weren't surprised when her eyes were dewy and she had a flushed face the next morning as they had seen many of Nolan's conquests look the same way.

One thing was for sure, Megan Atwood was falling for their oldest brother and it was only a matter of time before Nolan convinced her to return their land and reveal where their old homestead had been. The records from the land purchase would include all of the boundaries and once they had that, finding the treasure would be easy.

Blake and Teddy saw Megan's land and wealth as a way to remedy all of their problems. They could grow their herds ten times larger with her land to graze them. And once Nolan married her, he'd have access to all of her wealth, assuring them a steady stream of cash.

It was almost too good to be true. They openly joked about it in front of him, teasing him because he was finally in love. They encouraged him to spend time with her, hoping she'd fall in love with him. And if her sudden nervousness was any indication of that, he already had her in the bag. All they had to do now was sit back and count the money.

There was just one problem. They didn't know Nolan had changed his mind. He stopped caring about the old homestead and the treasure and was ready to abandon that dream and move on. After five years of searching, he had little to show for it, except for finding something he never even knew he wanted.

Nolan was trespassing on Bristol Bay Farms the day he found Megan alone and trapped in the woods. He thought about that day many times since then, turning it around in his head, trying to make sense of it. If his grandfather hadn't told him about the treasure, Nolan wouldn't have been there searching. Was that the real value of the treasure? Saving her life? Because that was the day he realized that he loved her.

And there was another confusing development. He found himself daydreaming about her and reliving the moments when she smiled at him. The only plotting that interested him was the one that ended with him kissing her. The fact that she didn't feel the same way about him was perplexing, but it wasn't enough to stop him from pursuing her. He couldn't just keep hoping she would fall in love with him too. He was going to have to openly court her in the way she deserved; with everything he had and with his whole heart. He couldn't hide behind polite talk and wishful thinking anymore. He needed to tell her in plain words that he loved her.

Blake and Teddy seemed supportive of him

pursuing a relationship with Megan but he suspected it was more out of greed than anything else. They weren't going to like it when he told them that he had other plans for their beautiful neighbor. He didn't want anything from her other than her love. And he didn't want to wait a minute longer to tell her.

NANCY DREW AND her crew were taking a well-deserved break, relaxing in the cool breeze off the ocean and having sweet tea on the veranda. They'd pulled their chairs closer to each other so they could rehash what they already knew about the crate in the attic and plan their next move. Megan was noticeably quiet, ignoring their chatter and her tea.

Luke noticed a cloud of dirt billowing up in the distance and pointed at it. "Hey, does anybody else see that? That's a car over there, speeding on that old dirt road. Can't they see it's not paved? It's not Jeff or Howard because they'd be driving a Bristol Bay Farm truck."

"Who do you think died?" Kate asked. "Do we know anyone who's been sick?" They all shook their heads and there was some low murmuring.

"Why would you think someone died?" Megan asked.

Felicity smiled. "Because that's the only time someone drives fast on that old road. It's full of potholes. Who wants to bet they blow a tire?"

"I'll take bets that they'll ruin their suspension," Luke countered. "And I'm not giving them a tow or driving them to town."

"I'll take that bet," Felicity laughed. "I've always loved this game with you all acting so callous about not helping someone in need."

"Honey, that's not someone who needs anything more than a decent head on their shoulders," Kate dryly told her. "I'm not moving off this chair, even if they're bleeding."

Megan nodded. "Why *are* you so tired all the time, Kate? Do you have a side hustle on top of our food truck side hustle?"

Kate stifled a yawn. "No, I'm too tired to think about anything but that crate in the attic. Maybe we should ask Aunt Alice about it."

Megan jumped off of her lounge chair and grabbed Kate, spinning her in a big hug. "I love you, Kate! You're so smart. I'm going to call her right now."

Megan disappeared inside to call Alice but was back before anyone had time to place another bet.

"What'd she say?" Felicity asked.

"Didn't pick up so I left her a nine-one-one message. She'll be out here. How far away is the car now?" she asked Luke.

"Maybe four, five miles. You have to really want to come here to get off the main road and drive another ten miles down that dirt road. Wonder who it could be?"

The veranda was quiet for a few minutes while they all held their thoughts to themselves. The car veered off the road and stopped.

Luke groaned. "What do you think it was? Tire? Steering? Suspension?"

"Does anyone want to take a bet that they're lost?" Megan asked.

Low murmuring and they all started emptying their pockets. By the time they were done, there were a total of fourteen bets. As far as Megan was concerned, the day just couldn't get any better.

"Who wants to bet that they call their motor club instead of walking the last miles?" Kate asked. Low murmuring and more money on the table.

Luke pointed back toward the road. "Now look at that. A bigger cloud of dirt is coming so it's probably Jeff and Howard in a truck this time." He let out a loud groan. "Shoot, they're going to pick up that driver and bring them here. I'm going to the barn and check on Elsa."

"Me too," Felicity chimed in.

"Oh no, you're not," Megan warned them. "Everyone's staying here. I might have been away for a while but I'm the one who started this game. The first one off the veranda wins and I can see right now that I'm going to be the last one here. No one gets to leave. That's final."

Kate winked at Megan. "You might want to go upstairs and freshen up. And by that I mean you should put on one of your low cut tops and some lipstick. And take off those horrible khaki pants. I'm going to burn them. You can thank me later."

"I can thank you now because when my mom gets here, I'll get something better than her normal disapproving looks. Should I put on the white top?"

"No, the sheer pink one. It's my favorite and that's saying a lot because I've been through all your clothes. You need to go shopping someplace better next time or let your mom buy all your clothes. I like what she picks for you because the colors are good on me," Kate told Megan with an approving nod.

Megan was forced to admit that Kate was right. "The next time you see my mom, you should tell her that you like her taste in clothes and I bet she'll shop for you too. I'll be back in a minute. How long before they all get here? Don't we need to get out cookies or something since it looks like we're having company?"

Luke didn't even pretend to be worried. "You have plenty of time to change. Let's just see who turns up before we start setting out a buffet. We'll wait here for you."

Megan rushed upstairs, throwing off her

zookeeper outfit, and selected a tiny pair of jean shorts and the pink top that Kate recommended. She splashed a little water on her face, put on mascara and lipstick, and bounded down the stairs.

"Anything new?" Megan asked as she settled back on her lounge chair. Felicity silently pointed toward the road while stifling a laugh.

"A third car?" Megan smiled. "Is it always this much fun when you sit on the veranda?"

Kate nodded. "The veranda has four sides so it kind of depends on where you're sitting. I like the water view myself but it's pretty entertaining on this side today."

Megan was overflowing with excitement. "Do we have binoculars? Maybe we can see who it is."

Luke pulled his hat down a little tighter on his head. "Why? They'll get here. They always do."

"The binoculars wouldn't work anyway, Megan," Felicity volunteered. "Trees line both sides of that road. Grandma Coleen had them put in seven years ago. She thought it would make it look homier. I think she saw a picture somewhere but I personally think the trees are beautiful."

Megan nodded. "You're right. But we can't ever pave that road because the dust cloud is like an early warning system. Who wants to bet that the third car is my mom?"

Kate smiled and nodded. "I'll take that bet and raise you that Aunt Alice will beat all of them to the house. You sent her a nine-one-one, right?"

Megan sighed. "Yes. That was me. Darn, it seemed like a good idea at the time."

Kate patted Megan's arm. "Don't worry. She knows that road better than anyone alive. I'm getting some more glasses and another pitcher of sweet tea. Our guests are bound to be thirsty."

"I'll help you," Megan volunteered as she started to get up.

Kate raised her eyebrows and gave her a long stare.

Megan shrugged. "Or I can sit here and wait for my mom. But call me if you need any help, Kate. This is so much fun."

Felicity smiled at Megan. "Well, you're the one who brought the fun. It was never like this before you came."

Megan waited to see if Felicity was going to laugh like she'd made a joke. But she just continued to stare at the car speeding toward them. No one had ever told Megan that she was funny or entertaining or even slightly amusing.

"What was it like before I came?" she asked them.

"Boring," Felicity said flatly.

"Quiet," Luke sighed.

"Stressful," Kate hollered from the kitchen.

"Glad I could make a difference," she told them. And then her heart swelled with all the love she felt for the little family she had here at Cove House. She should have done this a long time ago.

CHAPTER FOURTEEN

Alice Atwood received Megan's nine-one-one emergency message while she was at Jameson House, finishing up some details with her brothers. She took one look at her phone and immediately tried to call Megan back. When there wasn't an answer, she grabbed Chelsea and hurried her to the car.

"Now, I want you to call Luke and your cousins while I drive," she told Chelsea. "And don't stop trying until you reach one of them, sweetheart. I don't know what I would have done if you weren't right there to help me. I probably would have driven this car into a ditch."

"I know, Aunt Alice. So lucky. But after we get there and find out that everything's okay, I'm going to connect your car to your phone."

"Oh, I know how to do that, Chelsea. I guess I

just wanted a little company for the drive. Megan's never sent me a text like this before."

Chelsea stared unblinking at the road. "Aunt Alice, do you think we're driving a little fast?"

"Put on your seatbelt, honey. I could crash this car into a brick wall and we wouldn't get a scratch on us."

Chelsea winced. "But that's not going to happen, is it?"

Alice shook her head. "Never had a single accident in my whole life that I can remember. Maybe a few speeding tickets along the way but that's why I married your Uncle Walter. You can never have too many lawyers in the family. Did you reach someone at Cove House?"

"Still trying, Aunt Alice. Maybe they're all outside with the new calf?"

Alice shook her head. "Luke would have his phone if they were in the barn. My guess is that someone is hurt and they're all trying to stop the bleeding. I took a first aid course and that's why Megan called me."

Alice slowed the car a little to turn onto the entrance road. "Oh good, now I can floor it," she said.

Chelsea gripped the armrest and closed her eyes, praying that one way or another, it would be over soon.

The car swerved, hit a small bump and Alice

groaned. "Some idiot wrecked their car over there but it looks like Jeff and Howard are helping them. How do you like those boys? Are they working out?"

"Yes, Aunt Alice, they're wonderful," Chelsea replied in a shaky voice. "Talented, hard-working young men which we seem to have an overabundance of nowadays. Believe me, I'm not complaining. I guess they're a lot like lawyers. You can't have too many."

Alice nodded in agreement while she checked her lipstick in the rearview mirror, snapping it back in place when she'd finished. Chelsea momentarily had the urge to tell her that there was a mirror behind the sun visor but forgot all about it when the car swerved to avoid another pothole.

"Oh, look! I can see everyone's sitting on the veranda and no one's bleeding. I'm so happy, so glad we're finally here," Chelsea told Alice with a little sob.

"I know, dear. I'm happy too. Now, we should find out what this emergency is all about."

When Megan saw her mother get out of the car she ran to her. "You came so fast! Thanks, Mom. We've run into a puzzling thing in the attic. Well, the attic itself is puzzling too. Have you ever been up there?"

Alice's forehead wrinkled in confusion. "You

mean the metal room with a box? Sure, I've seen it. Grandma Coreen showed it to me. Is there a problem with it? I was told by the contractors that it was water-resistant and due to some special kind of a ventilation system, it was heat resistant too."

Megan exhaled deeply and relaxed her shoulders. "You don't know how relieved I am. Thank God. I should have called you hours ago when we were up there trying to figure it out."

Alice shrugged. "I didn't say that I know what it is. No one does. That's why I had experts look at it. Grandma Coreen was hoping it was a time machine." She brought her hand to her lips and her face turned sad. "I miss her."

Everyone turned to watch the red Bristol Bay Farm truck pull up to the house. Both doors for the front seat flew open and two men jumped out. Alice unabashedly hurried to them.

"Boys, this is Megan, your boss. I'm not sure what the emergency is but grab your bags and then you can get settled in." Alice beamed a smile at them and they smiled back. They took off their hats and came over to Megan.

"Megan, honey, this is Jeff. And he's a real sweetheart with his dark eyes and his...smile."

Alice cleared her throat before she continued. "He's going to bring some horses over for you to ride. I asked him to ride with you, not to keep you company or anything like that, but just to watch out for wild animals. I knew you wouldn't want to ride with a rifle. And after your romp in the woods, I decided to make sure you weren't in any danger while you were out exploring. I'd like you to get out and see the land here. It's an incredible place, Megan. But you need to see it with your own eyes."

Alice rested her hand on Megan's back and gave her a tiny nudge.

"Nice to meet you, Jeff, and with that introduction, I know I'm not ever going to forget you or your name," Megan told him with an amused look on her face.

"And this is Howard. He's a plumber and an electrician. His brother is a detective for the state of Virginia so he knows everything about security. I don't think he's a troublemaker but you'll want to keep an eye on him anyway. He's an open book, but I heard there aren't many nursery rhymes in that book."

Megan bit her lip, trying to keep a straight face when she noticed that Howard met and kept her gaze. Her mother should have also mentioned he wasn't shy. Or maybe this is what a man looks like when he's an open book.

"That's quite an introduction, Howard. You should know that my mother isn't usually this complementary. We're happy to have you," Megan told him.

The back seat door opened and everyone

turned to look at the driver who wrecked their car. Luke, the one most likely to be asked to help the driver, used the distraction and tried to escape to the barn. But Megan stopped him with a strong shake of her head. And then she heard her mother gasp.

"What in the Sam Hill are you doing here, Steve Richards? You've got a lot of nerve to show your face here," Alice scolded him, her voice going up two octaves.

Steve put up his hands like he was being held at gunpoint. "I just came to talk to Megan. I don't have anything to say to you, Alice."

"Oh, really? Did you think you were gonna sashay in here and monopolize my daughter's time? She's a busy woman. Next time, call ahead."

A rider approached from the west pasture, taking everyone's attention away from Steve. Chelsea took a wobbly step over to Megan. "Is this what I've been missing? Someone should have told me. It just might be worth the terrifying ride over here...and almost dying. Do you know who that man is? The man on the horse?"

Megan shrugged. "He might be my boyfriend. I'm not sure yet."

Chelsea nodded. "Nice."

Nolan stopped short, reining in his horse, and dismounted. "What's going on? Are you alright, Megan?"

Cove House

She started to speak but was interrupted by Steve. "Oh great, another beefed-up cowboy on steroids. What's going on here? Are you holding auditions?"

Chelsea nodded at Steve. "You could call it that. What's your problem, anyway? I thought Aunt Alice told you to leave."

"Okay, you just need to mind your own business. I wasn't talking to you and you're never going to be a part of this conversation," Steve angrily told her.

Nolan walked up to Steve, clearly displeased. "Where I'm from, we don't yell at women like that, but we were also taught to respect our elders. So, which is it going to be, old man? Because if you yell at her again, we're just gonna have to go somewhere private and have words. Do you understand? Lower your voice and be respectful to the lady."

Steve shook his head and turned back to Megan. "We can't have an intelligent conversation with all these people here. Where can we go to be alone?"

Megan narrowed her eyes and backed away. Sensing that he was losing her, Steve began pleading his case.

"Megan, I've had a lot of time to think about us, and mainly about you, and I've realized that I can't exist without you. You have to know that you

157

were the best thing to ever happen to me and how we ever gave up on each other is still bewilders me. I think we got caught up in something and then we felt like we had to see it through. But it wasn't good for either of us, Megan. Look at what's happened to you. You're stuck out here in the country and I might as well be dead, as horrible as I've been feeling. I can't go on without you. I love you so much, Megan. And I know you love me too. Isn't that why people stay together? For love?"

Alice took a steady look at her daughter. "How long are you going to stand there and let him keep talking? All that dribble coming out of his mouth is going to make me faint."

"It's okay, Mom," Megan reassured her. "Let him finish. I want to hear what he has to say. That's fair, right?"

Steve smiled at her. "It's one of the things I've always loved about you, Megan. You're so fair and kind-hearted."

Steve reached out and took Megan's arm. "Come on. I need to speak to you in private."

Alice narrowed her eyes at Steve. "Keep your entitled narcissistic troll hands off of my daughter."

Steve released Megan and focused his rage on Alice. "It made me sick to watch how you manipulated Megan and I bet you're already back to it. Is that why she's out here in the country hosting Magic Mike auditions? Because there's no other way to explain these three Rambo stooges and Roy Rogers over there. What's with those hats anyway? Are all of you prone to sunstroke or something?"

Alice wasn't going to let this go on one second longer. "You're crazy if you think I'm going to stand here and let you try to ruin my daughter's life again. I should have stopped it the first time you weaseled into her life."

"Me?" Steve glared at Alice. "You think I ruined her? That would almost be laughable if it didn't show just how blind you are to your own daughter's feelings. Because she was scared of her own shadow when I met her, all worried about what her mother would think. You put so many rules on her that she was frozen in fear."

Alice laughed. "If anyone was frozen, it was you. I saw your cold heart the day I met you and prayed she'd see it too. But she's always looked for the good in everyone and God knows, she must have had to look a long time to find any good in you."

"See? You just proved my point. And that's exactly why I had to keep you and all your underhanded meddling away from her. You Southern women, with all your polite talk. Half the time you're insulting people with your, *Bless your heart, honey,* and all the other ways you put good hard-working people down. But then, you look down your nose at everyone, including your daughter."

Megan shook her head. "Steve, you might as well stop right now because there's nothing left for us to say to each other. I don't need to talk to you now or for the rest of my life."

Steve's mouth dropped but he recovered quickly. "I can explain everything if we can just get away from here," he pleaded.

"No. You already know that I found the house, I found her, I found the baby. And, truthfully, I felt sorry for her because she was so young and trusting. I saw everything, so there's no way you can lie about it. I think we're done talking."

Steve shook his head and held out his arms to her. "No, Megan. You're so wrong. It's not what you think at all. I did it for one of my clients because he couldn't put the house in his name and that was his fiancé, not mine. His baby, not mine. I swear it wasn't my baby, Megan."

Megan nodded, rubbing the heel of her hand against her forehead. "The part about the baby? Well, that might actually be true. Did you do a DNA test? What did it feel like when you found out that she'd been lying to you? Bet you didn't like it very much."

"None of that is important now," Steve pleaded with her. "We have our whole lives ahead of us and a chance to do it right this time."

Megan sighed. "I'm still amazed at how stupid you think I am, Steve. I don't know what else to tell you other than I'm never coming back."

"If you'll just give me some time, we can work this all out. Come on, Megan. I know you can't be happy here."

Megan frowned at him. "At first, I was obsessed with finding out the truth. And now that I know what's true and what's a lie, you seem small and sad and the only thing I feel for you is regret and disappointment. I used to spend my time going through every day of our lives, trying to track when you started lying to me and then I realized that there wasn't just one lie. It was all a lie. It's just the way you are."

"Don't you see what your mother's doing to you?" Steve pleaded.

"All my mother did was bring me here and put me back on the land that's been in our family for generations and that's something you'll never understand. Having a foundation like this and a way to connect honestly with other people is worth a million times more than anything we had. Looking at it now, I don't know why I ever settled for the drab stifled existence we had."

Steve tried to reach for her again but this time Nolan stepped in. "Sorry, no more grabbing. I feel like someone should have taught you manners," he told Steve while shaking his head.

Megan pointed her finger at Steve. "And all those slurs you made about Southern women? Well, I'm a Southern woman and I guess I'm gonna have to tell you, *Bless your heart, you tried your best but it's not good enough.*"

Megan stopped long enough to look at the faces around her. She wasn't embarrassed that they'd heard about her divorce and were witness to the pathetic man she'd married. She felt love and support from them. She felt accepted.

Megan sighed, weary of Steve's presence. She thought she would feel intense fury if she ever saw his face again but instead, she felt nothing.

"This is the last time we're ever going to see each other and the last time I'll ever even think about you. You might want to look around because I have a family and that's ten times better than a restraining order. Walk back to your car, call a tow truck, and wait there. And I hope you didn't hit one of our beautiful trees."

As Megan walked into the house, she thought about Steve, with their bland khaki lifestyle and the starter home and the way he always made her feel like she wasn't good enough for him. She'd felt more alive in the last few months than she ever had in her entire sixteen years with him.

And then she realized that the fear she'd felt was gone. Her future had seemed uncertain but now she could finally see a clear path in front of her, a path leading directly to Nolan. It was about time that she started taking risks and he might just be the best risk out there. She smiled when she realized he was following her into the house. Well, he was certainly the best-looking risk.

CHAPTER FIFTEEN

*N*olan wasn't a simple man or even a man who could be easily satisfied. So when he looked at Megan's angelic face, he was confused. Not because he was waking up in her bed. Confused because he'd gone the whole night without even kissing her.

Maybe his brothers were right about her being different from other women. He certainly had different feelings when it came to her. He just wished she would hold still long enough for him to pin her down and find out if she had feelings for him too.

The first time he met her, she was in his face, waving her finger and threatening him. Then the night she'd spent at the ranch with him, she was a sobbing puddle of girlish mush who ended up being wildly entertaining. Then at Cove House, she was reserved but cold, probably from wearing all those sheer nightgowns.

If forced, he would describe her as unpredictable. And after he saw how decisively she dismissed her ex-husband, he knew he only had one chance to get it right.

He didn't want Megan in the usual way that he wanted a woman. He was ready to commit to her if she would just give him a sign, anything to show him that she saw him as someone who was more than a friend. He'd thought she was holding back because she wanted to take things slowly. But after yesterday, he realized it could also be because she was busy considering her options.

Those options were twentyish-aged men with solid jaws and broad shoulders, who were conveniently located near if not in her bedroom. He'd only been to Cove House once before and had innocently assumed that the men who worked there would be older than him. Although he'd never minded competition before, their close proximity to her put them at an advantage. An advantage that he had to eliminate.

In the predawn light, he put his arm around Megan and pulled her a little closer until her head was on his shoulder, closed his eyes, and waited. He listened to her breathing, waiting for a clue that she was awake but the gentle rhythm of it put him back to sleep.

The next time he opened his eyes, Megan standing next to the bed and smiling at him. "Oh good, you're finally awake." She walked barefoot onto the bed, holding a mug and a plate over her head. When she reached him, she carefully lowered herself to the bed and sat cross-legged.

"How'd you sleep? Do you want coffee, because I brought you some? And an omelet too. Do you want some juice?" she asked while offering him the mug.

"No, what I really want is a kiss," he answered.

She acted like it was a regular thing for them, leaning over him to place the coffee on the bedside table and giving him a light kiss on his lips before sitting back on the bed.

Nolan motioned for her to come back and she sweetly shook her head. "That was your good morning wish and you only get one. I put cheese on your omelet. I mean, I asked Kate to put cheese on it. She makes the best cheesesteak omelet with sweet onions, mushrooms, and green peppers. I can get you a plain one if this seems like too much. But it's almost noon so I thought you'd be hungry."

Nolan groaned and rubbed his eyes. "It's almost noon? What did you do to me last night?"

Megan's face went serious and she lowered her voice. "I might have talked your ear off. I woke you up a few times but finally gave up around midnight. Kate served some killer barbecue last night and you were ravenous. I think you fell asleep because Kate puts a little something extra in everything she cooks. Her food has that effect on me too. But you'll figure it out after a few meals. It's like being on a cruise. You have to pace yourself."

"You like going on cruises?" Nolan asked as he propped himself up on his elbows.

"I might if I didn't get seasick so easily. I've just heard that the food is great. But then, the food is also great here and I can eat and look at the ocean at the same time. I guess it might be as close to a cruise as I'll ever get," Megan told him while pushing her silky hair behind her ears.

"What time do you start giving afternoon wishes?"

Megan laughed. "That's crazy. Everyone knows that afternoon wishes were outlawed during the prohibition. They brought back alcohol but no one dared to bring back afternoon wishes. Do you want some juice?"

"No, I like it when you talk to me. Keep doing that while I eat."

"Oh, so you want me to entertain you? Sure. I can go over some things you missed last night while you were pretending to be awake. And I have a few dilemmas that I can talk about while you sit there and eat. Do you want to do that?"

Nolan took the plate from her and nodded.

Megan's face became animated, her eyes sparkling every time she looked at him. "So, with the Farm to Fork business. Chelsea thinks we should go to just one spot in the morning. Lisa, my friend at the library, said we could use the parking lot there. There are concerns that the truck will generate a traffic jam and we don't want to interfere with people trying to shop downtown.

Luke wants to make deliveries but I think that should happen only if a restaurant makes a large and standing order. And maybe we can take pre-orders from businesses and individuals too. What do you think?"

Nolan stopped, a forkful of the omelet hanging midair. "I don't know enough to have an opinion. But it sounds like they're all good ideas. Why can't you do all of them and change if you need to?"

Megan nodded. "Noted. The second dilemma has to do with Jeff. You met him last night, remember? He's the one with the dark hair and eyes?"

Nolan's fork clattered to his plate. He'd noticed Jeff sneaking glances at Megan and smiling at her. "I've been meaning to ask you why you need so much help here. You have the bull and two cows now, but that's hardly enough to keep three men busy."

Megan's arms flew up. "Thank you! That's exactly what I thought. And then I saw the way

Chelsea was looking at him last night so I was considering moving her here from Jameson House and seeing how it worked out. My mom hired him to take me riding but, seriously, how much time can I spend on a horse?"

"Sure, sure," Nolan agreed as he set his empty plate on the bedside table. "So let's go back to the part where you said that your mom hired him? Did she hire Howard too?"

"Yes, but I don't blame her, Nolan. She wasn't happy with the way things were handled when you saved my life and she's been even more protective than normal, which I am completely fine with. If I fight her on anything, she'll send Walter out to talk to me and, let's just say, to put it mildly, that would be the end of me. And now, I've talked the whole time while you ate breakfast, just like I promised."

Nolan nodded. "And who's Walter?"

"Sorry. After last night, I feel like we've known each other for ages and I can't believe I forgot to tell you about Walter. He's my dad and just about the best person alive. I'd die if I ever disappointed him."

Megan grinned at him when she saw him try to stifle a laugh. "Okay, what's so funny?"

"Nothing is funny. I just was thinking that the next time I spend the night here, I'm going to wake up earlier so that you have more time to talk to me."

"Wow, next time? Aren't you getting a little too confident, Mr. Prescott?" Megan teased him.

Nolan solemnly took Megan's hand. "No, only submitting to the inevitable. You see, I love Kate's cooking and I won't be able to stay away."

Megan pulled her hand from him, stood up, and walked to the end of the bed, jumping onto the floor.

"Where are you going?" Nolan asked.

"To get Kate. I was going to offer to help you shower but now that I know you play favorites, I'll see if Kate is available." She kept a straight face but laughed as she tried to run by him. He caught her three steps from the open doorway and she didn't resist him when he took tomorrow morning's wish a day early.

FELICITY WAS UPSTAIRS, trying her best to avoid eavesdropping on Megan and Nolan. But the door was open and their voices were loud, not to mention all of their laughter. She was sitting in her usual spot, nestled in the pillowed window seat down the hall and around a corner from Megan's room. She could hear everything they said, unabashedly absorbing it like a dry sponge.

Her obsession with them started last night.

After the hoopla with Megan's ex-husband was over, everyone came inside and an impromptu party began. There were drinks and a big meal, with Aunt Alice being the center of attention. While everyone else at dinner was busy talking and eating, Felicity had kept quiet, concentrating on the only thing in the room that interested her; the seductively engrossing interaction between Megan and Nolan. Everyone had hinted that they were in a relationship after Megan spent the night at the Prescott ranch. But as Felicity watched them, there was more shyness than familiarity, like they were on a first date with each of them focused only on the other.

Even though Megan and Nolan were sitting across from each other at the large harvest table, they were still having their private conversation and successfully flying past the first stages of a courtship. Felicity watched with fascination as Megan and Nolan locked eyes and began flirting.

When Megan looked down, Nolan's eyes widened in fear. Megan shyly batted her eyelashes and Nolan's eyes twinkled with hope. And when she looked directly at him, his eyes glimmered happily. Felicity wished she had her sketchbook so she could capture every emotion on their faces.

Occasionally, someone would try to engage one of them in a conversation or ask them a question. And even though Nolan was talking to someone else, before he finished what he was saying, he'd always look at Megan and smile at her. Maybe he knew she'd be listening and watching him. And maybe she knew the same thing about him. Maybe it's what happens when two people are in love. It wasn't what they said, or even if they spoke to each other. It was the intense way that they paid attention to each other. Everyone else ceased to exist and they were alone in their private realm, sustained by their love and never taking their eyes off of each other.

Felicity's mother left when she was young and the little she could remember about her parents centered on a quiet coldness. And after her mother left, her dad gradually became more aloof and distracted. Her father wasn't a likable man to begin with but she hoped that somewhere deep inside him, there was kindness and possibly even love. But just like her mother, as soon as she was able, she left him too.

Grandma Coreen must have known that her oldest son, Bill, wasn't capable of raising his daughter by himself and she kept a close eye on Felicity. More times than not, she came to get Felicity from daycare and she always kept her during the summer when Bill was the busiest. It went on like that until Felicity turned five and Grandma Coreen forgot to return her at the end of summer. As far as Felicity knew, no words were ever exchanged about it.

Grandma Coreen was the closest thing to a mother that Felicity had so when she realized that she was staying with her forever, her world changed from black and white and blossomed into full color.

Under her grandma's watchful eye, Felicity flourished. They both loved animals and adored horseback riding. She went to art classes and gymnastics. She played sports, made friends, and easily transitioned to life away at college. When her grandma died, it was the worst day of her life, even worse than the day her mother left.

And then Aunt Alice showed up, her motto being, take no prisoners. She tipped her magic wand and fixed everything, from squeaky floorboards to replacing whole buildings. Alice comforted Felicity with one hand and shoved her out the door with the other. She said that young women needed to try a little of everything before ultimately deciding on the life they wanted. And since the only life she'd ever wanted would have to involve Luke, she was stuck, unable to decide anything or even think about her future.

Grandma Coreen had told her that as she grew up, one day Luke would notice her. But one day turned into a year, and that turned into more years. Sometimes she felt like if she could just get his attention for one minute, he would see her.

It was her job to help with Elsa even though Luke hadn't ever actually let her do anything. And ever since the vet had removed the splints, Elsa was standing and acting like a normal frolicking calf. So Felicity's job was over along with her excuse to see Luke.

She made a deal with herself. She would go to the barn and give Luke one last chance. If he didn't look at her or smile, she wouldn't ever come back again. Now that she knew what she was looking for, she wasn't going to settle for anything less.

"Hello," Felicity waved and smiled at Luke. "I'm late today, checking on Elsa. Do you need any help with her?"

Luke didn't look at her. "Late?"

"Well, with all the excitement going on yesterday, I guess I didn't sleep that well," she told him while tossing her hair.

"That was something, right?" Luke mumbled absentmindedly.

"What did you think? I mean, was everyone paying attention, or was it just me?"

"I think Megan and her ex-husband were center stage," he said, chuckling. "I don't know how anyone could've missed it."

"I know, but aren't you proud of Megan? It sounded like he cheated on her. I can't believe that someone did all that to her and she didn't even seem angry. Weren't you surprised?"

Luke shook his head. "I don't like to get involved with things like that and I'm the last person who'd know how someone's supposed to act. One thing for sure though, I'm never going to mess with Alice."

"That's because Aunt Alice knows exactly what she wants and I feel sorry for anyone who gets in her way, especially when she's made up her mind.

But I was wondering if you noticed how Megan and Nolan have become closer lately. Last night, they seemed like they were in their own little world."

Luke glanced up at Felicity, his brow furrowed. "Really? I wouldn't think those two could have anything in common. I heard Megan left Bristol Bay when she was eighteen and moved to New York City. She seems like the adventurous type and Nolan seems, well, like someone who's just discovered that his house is wired for electricity."

Felicity frowned. "You sound like you don't like him."

"I don't have any feelings about him, one way or another. People around town talk, and even though this is a small town, there's usually a grain of truth to everything that's said. I don't trust him or his brothers."

"That's odd because I think he's wonderful and he seems to like Megan. I mean, he can't take his eyes off of her," Felicity dreamily told him.

"I hate to tell you this, but not all men are honest with their intentions. Of course, he's paying attention to her. But I thought you would have already figured out why he's doing that."

"Figured out what, Luke?"

"Maybe you should ask Kate or Chelsea or even your dad. This is more of a family thing and I don't feel comfortable interfering or guessing at something when I don't really know."

"You don't have to tell me. Just tell me what your take is on it. Aren't you allowed to have an opinion? Even if you aren't a blood member of this family, I'm pretty sure that everyone thinks of you like family."

"Well, as long as you know that this is just speculation. I'm guessing, right? I don't know anything for sure but after Grandma Coreen died, first your Aunt Alice was out here giving orders, having everything fixed, and hiring a bunch of people. And immediately after that Megan shows up. But that wasn't the odd part. It turned weird when Alice dropped her off and never came back."

Felicity tilted her head quizzically. "I know what happened. But it all seemed normal to me. So, what does that mean to you?"

"It means that Megan took over that day and she's the new owner of Bristol Bay Farms. Alice was just waiting until Megan's divorce was final before bringing her here. And I'm positive that those Prescott boys noticed too. Nolan, the oldest one? You haven't detected how he's basically laid claim to her and swaggers around here like he already owns the place? How are you going to feel when he moves in and takes over?"

Felicity didn't know what to say. She was raised and loved by her grandmother who taught her that people were fundamentally good. She didn't see the sinister ulterior motives that Luke saw when he looked at Nolan Prescott. "Why do you think he has to have an ulterior motive? Why can't he be falling in love with Megan? What's wrong with you?"

A look of surprise crossed Luke's face. "What are you talking about, Felicity?"

Felicity clenched her teeth, huffing as she took a last look at Luke. His head was back down and he was busy working on something for the Farm to Fork business that was scheduled to start the next day.

"I don't think you know anything about this. Why can't Megan have a man who wants to be with her, just for who she is and not for what she has? I think you're jaded, Luke. And it makes me sad. I don't even know when you got this way," she said stiffly.

Felicity left the barn, marched to the house, and went straight to her bedroom. There was a long summer ahead to fill and she wasn't going to spend another minute moping inside the house feeling sorry for herself.

She was willing to settle for whatever stupid superficial thing that Luke said Megan had with Nolan. in fact, she was going to set out right now to do everything she could to make sure it happened.

She opened her closet door and started throwing clothes. When conducting a makeover, the first thing you do is change the way you think, and as of five minutes ago, she'd already done that. The next thing you do is change the way other people think about you. She was going to turn heads and get everyone's attention. She was going to start living the life she wanted, not the life she had.

CHAPTER SIXTEEN

Megan's morning had been filled with highs and lows. She had her high moment the first time she saw the Farm to Fork truck. It was the greenest, brightest, most unique vehicle that she'd ever seen. It was going to stand out like a glorious green thumb and the huge shiny silver letters would be visible from space, just as she'd planned. Even neighboring aliens deserved fresh food for their meals.

Most of the people from the neighboring farms brought their products to Cove House before dawn. Luke had already allotted, charted, and labeled all of the cargo areas so the loading of the truck went quickly and easily. Most of the contributors wanted to go the first day, turning the whole thing into a convoluted parade. That was Megan's low moment and she reluctantly elected to stay home. Kate promised to send her a text to let her know how everything was going but other than that, she wasn't expecting anyone that day.

By mid-morning, she'd showered and changed into a summery top and shorts and was sitting on her bed thinking about the crate in the attic. She opened the drawer on her bedside table and pulled out the old skeleton key for the attic, toying with it and toying with the idea of taking another look in the attic. She'd come tantalizingly close to opening the crate once before. There wouldn't be any interruptions today.

The worrying feeling that she'd initially had about the past remaining where it belonged was still there but it was diminished by the overwhelming need to know what was in that crate. That need pushed her forward and pushed her to unlock the door.

There was nothing sinister about it since her mom had admitted that she knew about it too. But there was still an overriding urge to open the crate. She reached for her phone and texted Howard, knowing that he was the only one who hadn't left Cove House.

When he knocked on the front door, she was already there waiting for him. "Are you sad that you were left behind, Howard?"

Howard laughed, his face relaxing into an easy smile. "Maybe a little, ma'am. But when a hundred more people arrived and I saw how crowded it was going to be, I decided to stay here. There's only so much room inside and everybody else is just going to be following in their cars. What about you, ma'am?" he asked Megan.

"I guess that I felt the same way. I've never been fond of crowds unless it's a sporting event. But I agree that there were too many people."

There was an awkward silence before Megan remembered that he didn't even know why he was here. "Of course, you're probably wondering what was so important that you had to come right now. I was hoping that you could take apart an old crate for me. You might want to take a look at it first because I couldn't begin to tell you what you'd need. I just want one side taken off, " she added.

Howard was quick to smile at her. Everything at Cove House was less work and more waiting, but he could manage a wood crate. "Do you mind if I take a look at it before I give you an answer?"

"Of course not. Follow me," Megan told while motioning for him to come into the house.

Howard followed her up the stairs, through her bedroom, and up the narrow stairs to the attic. When they reached the top, she gave him his own set of lights and as soon as they turned them on, she directed him to the crate.

"I get the feeling this has been up here for a long time, is that right?" he asked.

"Yes, one hundred years. At least that's what

the date on the crate implies. No one knows for sure."

"And you're positive you want to know what's inside? Have you wondered why no one has opened it all these years?"

"Sure. I've wondered but by the shape and size, there's every indication that it's just a piece of furniture. It wasn't uncommon back then for people to send furniture to their relatives in the United States."

Howard confidently walked toward the stairs, calling back to her as he went down, "I'll be back in a few minutes. It won't take long to take off one side. I don't imagine it would take more than a few minutes."

Megan went back to her room to check her phone for a message from Kate, the third time since this morning. She sighed and threw her phone in the drawer with the key. She'd get her phone as soon as she locked the attic door again.

With the house so empty and quiet, Megan didn't have to listen to know when Howard came back inside. She heard the metal clanging and thumping from cords bouncing on the hardwood floor long before he made it to her room. She got up from the bed to help him, only to see that he was carrying hammers, crowbars, tarps, extension cords, and lights. It was amazing how much he could manage with his big hands and shoulders.

Maybe her mom knew what she was doing when she hired him.

It was hard for Megan to hide her eagerness. "Can I help you with any of that?"

He grinned a little. "This is the kind of adventure that I love. I can't remember the last time I opened something when I didn't know what was going to be inside."

A perplexed look crossed Megan's face. "That's unusual. Don't you get Christmas or birthday presents?"

"Sure. But I have this uncanny ability to know what's inside the packages, all of the packages."

"That's not possible to always be able to do something. So you're telling me if I wrapped up something for you and wanted to give it to you as a present, you'd know what was inside?"

"Yes, that's exactly what I'm saying. My dad's the same way. And because we couldn't give each other a gift that would be a surprise, we started giving each other presents that we couldn't unwrap. And we've been giving each other the same pair of pants, back-and-forth every Christmas, for the last five years."

Megan gave him a puzzled look. "So you know you're getting the same pair of pants back from him that you gave him the year before? What's the fun in that? Don't the pants fit either of you?"

"I don't know," Howard admitted. "We've never

tried them on. The first year that he gave them to me, he wrapped them in plastic and then put them in a paint can and then filled the can with cement. Then he put it in a box with a big ribbon and put it under the tree. Do you have any idea how long it took for me to chip off all of that concrete? I was only nineteen at the time and I didn't want him to know that I couldn't figure out how to get the concrete off. And when I finally broke all the concrete, I realized there was a pair of pants in the paint can. It never occurred to me to keep them. I wanted to give the pants back to him, only in a wrapping that was harder than he gave me. I had to get creative."

Megan felt like she was six years old again and at the Public Library for Storytime. "You have to tell me what happened the next Christmas. I'll go crazy not knowing. Please?"

Howard pushed up his sleeves. "The next year, I took the pants and put them in a coffee can with millions of BBs. Then I took the can to a welder and had the lid welded shut. Then I had it crushed inside of a car. Imagine getting that for Christmas," he told Megan with a big infectious smile.

Megan laughed. "I can't tell if that is the meanest thing or the funniest thing I've ever heard. When I recover, I'd like to hear what happened to those pants after he got them out."

He raised one eyebrow and leaned toward her.

"Who said he got them out of the wrapping? He only had a year."

"So he didn't?"

Howard smiled, motioning toward the attic. "I'll tell you later if you want to know. How about we go up there and see what's in that crate?"

Megan reluctantly agreed. "But you have to tell me what happened because I have so many questions, like was it crushed inside of a Volkswagen?"

"Yes, I promise to tell you all about it but we need to get this equipment up to the attic. The staircase is too narrow so it has to be done piece by piece."

"Of course, maybe I can hand it up to you?" Between the two of them, they were able to drag all of the equipment to the attic. Megan plugged in the extension cords for the lights and Howard started dismantling the wooden crate.

After a few minutes, he stopped working. "There's packing material underneath the crate's wooden slats. It looks like cardboard and paper and maybe some wool or cotton padding. Do you want me to cut it or try to unwind it?"

Megan wasn't tall enough to reach the top of the crate. "I'm just going to have to take your word for what you see. I'd have to haul a step ladder up here and I doubt that it would fit up the stairs."

"I can't see it either but I can feel around the

perimeter of the packing material," Howard told her. "It seems to be all one piece instead of being stuffed along the inside of the crate in increments. As far as I can tell, the cardboard is the outer layer with paper in the middle and then the softer fabric padding directly on the piece of furniture."

Megan wasn't sure how to get it out. "What do you think, Howard? I don't want to tear it apart because I plan on putting it back together the way it originally was."

"I might be able to do that if I take off another side of the crate. Then I'll be able to find the starting place and unwind all the packing material. Is that alright with you?" he asked.

"That sounds good," Megan answered. Her stomach was in knots from excitement and she was glad she was getting to look at this without an audience. She didn't know what was in there, but it had to be something really special.

Howard pulled off the second side in one piece. "I think I'm getting the hang of it. Do you want the third side off? The crate is too close to the wall to get to the last side."

Megan found herself agreeing with him. When the third side came off, he was able to pull the padding without breaking it. They both stepped back.

"Wow," Howard marveled. "It's some kind of a writing desk. Hand-carved too." He pushed on the top of it. "It has a bookcase on top. It's two pieces."

Megan pointed to the middle section. "It's a secretary. That front part drops down for a flat working space. It's handpainted, very intricate."

The secretary had been painted a pale yellow with cerulean blue ornamental vining, running along the edges and circling on every surface. She guessed it was almost eight feet tall and four feet wide. The top bookcase was arched and had doors that opened from the center, swinging outward. The secretary itself had three drawers, curved legs, and black ornate hardware.

"Do you know anything about antiques?" Megan quietly asked Howard.

He shrugged. "Enough to know this was expensive a hundred years ago and that it's appreciated while it's been sitting up here. Who sent it?"

Megan slowly shook her head. "I don't know and there's no way to find out. I feel like we should open a bottle of wine and just..."

"Look at it?" Howard suggested.

"Yes, that's a wonderful idea. The wine is in the back of the kitchen pantry, left side. Bring two bottles so we don't have to mess with any glasses."

As soon as he left, Megan got to her feet, trying to look at it from the three sides that were uncovered. She tried to open the desk, but it was locked, which was agonizing as it was sure to have cubby holes and secret compartments under there. She tried the drawers but they were locked too. She'd come full circle and was back to looking for another key.

Out of frustration, she reached up and pulled on the doors to the bookcase. They opened, revealing stacks of papers and a leather-bound diary. When she heard Howard coming up the stairs, she quickly put the diary back and shut the doors.

Howard came up sideways through the stairs, carrying the bottles of wine. "How did it get even more gorgeous since I left? See all that carved molding? Are those wheat sheaves painted on there?"

"I thought that too. But after looking at all of the scenes painted on here, I realized that it's trees blowing in the wind. There's an intricate scene painted on the door fronts of the bookcase. It looks like two houses separated by water. It's such a beautiful and unexpected present."

Howard leaned forward. "Did you hear that? I think someone's calling you--there, I heard it again."

"This was too good to last," Megan told him as she reluctantly followed him out of the attic. She closed the door behind them and listened for her phone. "I don't hear it. Are you sure you heard my phone?"

Howard scowled. No, I'm sure I heard someone calling you, as in calling your name," he corrected her. "Is anyone else here?"

"I guess it's just the three of us," Nolan answered.

Megan was mid chug on her bottle when she was surprised by Nolan's voice. She sputtered a little and gasped for air. "Oh my gosh, is something wrong? Did someone get hurt already? I told Luke those apples needed to be better secured. I hope he remembered to get liability insurance."

Nolan pinched his eyebrows with one hand. "It looks like you're having a party. Do you mind if I stay?"

Megan shrugged and looked at Howard for support, but he looked as blank as she did. "You never answered my question, Nolan."

Nolan took off his hat and threw it on the bed. "Everything is fine. No emergency yet. Why don't we go downstairs and get something to eat? There has to be something left from last night."

Megan choked on the wine. "You need to warn me before you say something funny."

"But I didn't say anything funny," Nolan insisted. "I was just talking about finding the leftover food from last night."

"Well, Good luck with that. I've looked for leftovers every day since I moved here and the refrigerator is always empty. It's been my very own personal running joke. You're a genius If you can figure out what happens to the food around here. But Howard knows where the wine is kept. Do you want a bottle?"

"I guess. If you don't mind," he told Howard. "But check around the kitchen while you're there. There has to be something to eat."

As soon as Howard left, Nolan leaned closer to Megan. "I feel like you're up to something. What's going on?"

Megan innocently took another swig of wine. "Nothing's going on. Why do you ask?"

"No reason, I guess." Nolan sighed. "Maybe once I start drinking, I'll be able to catch up with the two of you and then you'll tell me what the big secret is. In the meantime, we should ditch Howard and find something fun to do, like strip poker."

She ignored his suggestion and held out the bottle of wine. "You just have to try this one because it's my favorite. Did I ever tell you that our vineyard is the best in the country?"

Nolan took a long drink and nodded in agreement. "You have more of this downstairs?"

"Yes. And that's where the playing cards are kept too. I have to warn you though. Stories that begin with drinking and gambling and women always end with a man being ruined."

He shrugged. "I'll take my chances."

Megan gave him a coy smile. "Are you sure that you want to play for clothing? Wouldn't you feel safer if we played for money?" She solemnly pointed to her two pieces of clothing and moved a step closer to him.

Nolan grinned, liking where this conversation was headed. "Don't you have something else on underneath there?"

Megan shook her head, a hint of a frown on her face. "You mean like another top and another pair of shorts?"

"Something like that. Why don't you send Howard to the store and we'll play strip poker up here?"

Megan winked at him. "It's so cute how you assume you're going to win. Meet you downstairs."

Nolan sat down on her bed and took another drink from the bottle. He came over as soon as Blake warned him that Megan was alone at Cove House with Howard. But he never expected to find them together and he certainly didn't expect to find them in Megan's bedroom. It looked like he was going to be chaperoning because he wasn't going to leave the two of them alone. He let out a long sigh and hoped the Farm to Fork truck was empty and headed back. It had already been a long day and it wasn't even noon yet.

CHAPTER SEVENTEEN

*A*s Felicity got closer to Pearls and Curls Salon, she noticed a crowd of women standing inside, tightly pressed against the windows. She barely got inside before Pearl motioned for her to sit in one of the salon's chairs.

"You come on over here, honey, and we'll get you settled. Do you still want the works?"

"Yes, I want a complete makeover. Top to toe, and anything else you have."   She wasn't exactly sure about what was included in that package but she figured it was about time she started trying too hard instead of never trying hard enough. "I hope you don't mind me asking, but why are they huddled around the window?"

"It's that new Farm to Fork truck that everyone's been waiting forever since we saw the flyers," Pearl sighed. "It's been like this all morning. Between everyone buying and everyone watching, the crowds never let up. I've never seen the Library parking lot so full. You'd think it was the Summer Olympics."

The Farm to Fork truck had created quite a commotion in downtown Bristol Bay. And the big plate glass windows on the front of the salon gave them a front-row seat to the pandemonium. Their scheduled customers had been showing up early for their appointments all morning long. Some of the regular customers were stopping by just to join in on the socializing. In any case, the word was out. Pearls and Curls Salon had the best view in town.

Gwen turned away from the window to get Pearl's attention. "I put up my sign in the store window saying I'd be back in twenty minutes and that was more than an hour ago. Do you think I should be getting back?"

"I don't think anyone's gonna notice," Pearl answered. "Too bad your store isn't located closer to the library because you'd be bursting with all kinds of business right about now."

Pearl's sister, Carla, brought Felicity a bright pink smock to put on over her clothes. "You sit tight, honey. You're going to walk out of here looking like a new woman."

Sisters Carla and Pearl had owned Bristol Bay's best beauty salon for the last twenty-six years. Not only was it the best place to indulge in one of their many salon services, but it was also the best place to get together with other like-minded women and gossip.

Carla pointed to the bright green truck. "Marjorie Peters was saying those boys are selling their grass-fed beef directly to customers on their website."

"Did I hear you say that they have a website?" Jeannie Williamson used her elbows to break free of the crowd by the windows. "I bet it's called the beefy boy's website."

"Now, you stop all that talk about beef. What's wrong with those good looking ranchers tapping into a market where they'll be appreciated?" Pearl asked with an evil grin on her face.

Gwen agreed. "There's no denying that they'll be in high demand."

"What's going to be in high demand?" Carla wisecracked. "The beef or those boys?"

Pearl held up her hands to shush the ladies. "No more talking about beef. We're ladies. Unless someone wants to comment on the high quality of their beef."

Felicity sat there in the styling chair wearing her bright pink smock and listened to everything they said. Even though she wasn't part of the Farm to Fork premier, she was taking mental notes on all the fuss that the truck had generated. She hadn't expected that there would be so much excitement from the women in town.

"What's everyone looking at now?" Felicity asked Pearl.

"Oh, it's just those Prescott brothers. Two of them are down there at that food truck selling beef jerky and their grass-fed beef. The salon has a clear shot to the library's parking lot and as long as that food truck keeps parking there, we can see everybody coming and going. They've been busy like that all morning. I can't imagine they still have anything left to sell."

Gwen added, "I heard they sold out of their beef jerky an hour ago. Some of the ladies over at the café have been calling it hunky jerky. We were thinking about contacting Blake and asking if he wanted to use that name as his trademark."

"Once word got out that we have the best view in town, the ladies have just been flocking in here," Pearl said. "Jeannie, why don't you go over there and buy something from Blake so he can carry it to your car? I want to see him walking again."

She turned back to Felicity. "So you were wanting highlights and a trim? We have a special this week on wraps and packs. And you need to come back next week. We hired this girl from Richmond who's a certified eyelash technician. I heard she's really good although I don't know why she'd want to move here without even knowing anyone."

Felicity needed Pearl to focus on her. "Of course, it's always difficult starting over in a new town but I'm sure she has her reasons. I just need to ask you something important before you start. I'm going to be blonde when this is over, right?"

Pearl shook her head. "Honey, we're not turning your hair blonde, we're just giving you heavy, heavy highlights which means it's not blonde. You're too sweet of a girl for that. Just brightening you up a bit. Do you understand the difference?"

Felicity solemnly nodded. "You just have to promise me that I'll look different. Really different. So different that no one will recognize me when I walk out of here."

"Honey, no one's going to recognize you because of the way you walk and the way you keep your head up high," Pearl told her. "Because that's how everyone feels when I'm done with them."

Felicity had never seen so many of Bristol Bay's women congregate in one place other than church, of course. She'd always thought that these ladies subsisted on only pure thoughts. But it turned out that she was wrong. Very wrong. All she wanted to do was cover her ears but between the scissors and the substantial highlights she was getting in her hair, it wasn't possible.

Paula Myers was the first to grab her purse and head over to the library parking lot. Everyone crowded around the window watching as she got Blake to come out of the truck and carry her packages. The women at the window cheered while Felicity sunk lower in her chair.

WHEN THE TRUCK and everyone from Cove House hadn't returned by noon, Megan went into the kitchen looking for something to make for the three of them. There was plenty of fresh meat and seafood in the meat cooler and the pantry was stuffed with fresh vegetables.

Even though she had everything she would need to make a meal, she would be doing it reluctantly. She didn't know when it happened, but at some point, cooking lost its charm and she approached it with the same enthusiasm as she did when she had to do other meaningless chores.

They've been playing strip poker for an hour and she was the only one who still had on all of her clothes. Nolan and Howard were uncomfortably sitting at the dining room table and she needed to find some excuse to put all this torture to an end. She was positive that if the roles were reversed they wouldn't continue to let her suffer either.

"Does anyone want me to cook something for lunch?" she called through the closed door. "And if you say yes, you have to put your clothes on before I come back in there."

She heard chairs moving, some talking that she couldn't make out, and then Nolan came through the door still buttoning his shirt. "I thought you said you didn't like to cook?"

"Not liking something and being able to do something are two different things. Are you hungry or not? Because we have everything from shrimp to steak and anything you can think of to accompany it. I was thinking something we could do quickly, like steaks?"

Nolan buttoned his shirt cuffs and didn't look up at her. At least she knew one thing for sure. The best way to keep a man from looking at her with adoring eyes was to beat him at poker. "I'd eat anything right about now," he told her. "Even something you'd cook for me."

"That was charming," she remarked. "Did you have to stay up all night trying to think of something sweet to say to me? Or are you a sore loser?"

"Actually, I didn't even know that I was going to see you today. But then I'm beginning to realize that everything about you is unexpected. I'm not pouting, I'm just trying to keep up."

"Do you want to ask Howard what he'll eat?"

Nolan gave her a sheepish grin. "I can't go back in there. I'd be much happier if I never had to see him again for the rest of my life. I'm too old for this."

"That's hysterical because this was your idea, remember? Why don't I make something and surprise you? It'll have to be something quick but if you are as hungry as I am you shouldn't care."

"I can pick out food if you'll cook it. You have to remember that I live with my two brothers. None of us has eaten anything green in months."

Nolan selected something to grill from the meat cooler and she chose a variety of vegetables that would work for a salad. When she went out to the dining room to ask Howard if he wanted a salad, he was gone.

"Okay Nolan, what'd you say to Howard to scare him away?"

"Howard was on a losing streak. If he left, it was purely for self-preservation, not because of anything I said to him. I certainly hope he hasn't heard about workplace sexual harassment because I'd hate it if I had to testify against you."

Megan turned to face Nolan, her hands on her hips. "I wasn't alone with him. You were. If anyone sexually harassed him it was after I came into the kitchen. I'm sure you scared him with all of all your stupid grinning that just got worse the more clothes you took off."

"That's because I knew your luck couldn't hold for very much longer. I was looking forward to seeing what was on underneath your blouse."

"I don't know if I should be disappointed or flattered. Or just chalk it up to your inexperience with women," she teased him. "You know we can take off our bras without removing clothing, don't you?"

"I didn't know that but I'd be happy if you wanted to show me sometime." He leaned closer to her and put his hand on her waist. "Maybe the next time we play poker and Howard isn't sitting there watching?"

"I'm kind of surprised that you're even considering playing cards with me again."

"Is that a challenge, Megan?" He moved closer and slid his hands to encircle her waist. "Because we could play now, just the two of us, and I might try to win."

"Such a gentleman. You pretended to lose so you could spare me the embarrassment of removing my clothes?" she taunted. "Or is it just that you don't like to share?"

"Sharing, I guess. Howard seems like he could take a hint. He would have left before you had the chance to remove anything."

"Well, he left hungry so we should make extra. You raise cattle, does that mean you know how to cook it? Because I'm starting a salad and I like my meat rare. Less talking and more cooking," she ordered him.

They took their food to the dining room and got out another bottle of wine to go with it. Nolan was just getting comfortable being alone with her when one of Bristol Bay's red jeeps pulled up and skidded to a stop. Megan looked away from her food for a second and then continued eating.

"Do you know who that is?" Nolan asked her.

"Yes, it's blonde Felicity in a short blue sundress. Tight too. Good for her," Megan said approvingly. "I never took her for a Princess Barbie Boutique Girl but it looks good on her. Who knew that she even had legs?"

Nolan chuckled. "Look who else noticed that she has legs. Could Howard move any faster?"

Felicity's dress was tight everywhere but at the hem, which meant that every little breeze was tossing her skirt in a playful peek-a-boo Marilyn Monroe-esque way. While she was trying to hold it down, Howard was trying to hold all of her shopping bags in his arms.

Megan couldn't have been happier. Seeing that Felicity was finally coming out of her shell was a relief because, even though she'd been tempted, she didn't want to intervene.

The Farm to Fork truck pulled up next to Felicity and a worried Luke was the first to get out. Megan pulled at Nolan's shirt cuff. "Pay attention. This is about to get very interesting."

"What is...oh crap. What's wrong with Luke's

face?" Nolan turned in his chair to watch the drama as it unfolded.

"I wish we could hear what everyone's saying. Should we go out on the veranda?" Megan asked. "Maybe we could hear better out there."

"No," Nolan advised her. "We want to stay far away from that. I hope she knows what she's doing."

"She does," Megan answered. "Finally. It took her forever to figure Luke out. All she had to do was get his attention."

"Is that what you did?" Nolan asked with a quizzical look. "You didn't come to the ranch half-naked hoping I'd notice, did you?"

"God, you're cute, but kind of dumb sometimes," her blue eyes sparkled with mischief. "I couldn't have planned that in a million years. That was fate and her tricky fingers, not me. I should have paid attention and maybe she wouldn't have left me in the forest for you to find. I could have made it so much easier on myself if I wasn't so stubborn. I guess that makes me the dumb one, doesn't it?"

Nolan listened to her words but only heard her saying that she loved him. All of this time, he'd been waiting for a sign. When, in the end, all he had to do was ask her. It was just that simple.

When he stood up and offered his hand, she smiled at him. "It's about time. I didn't think you'd ever ask."

CHAPTER EIGHTEEN

*M*egan woke up with a smile on her face. It was her turn to go with the Farm to Fork truck today and Nolan was going with her. Last night, everyone got together and decided they had to end the carnival atmosphere in the Library parking lot. The truck could only hold a limited number of salespeople and the rest who followed along just added to the traffic jam that was clogging the library parking lot. So, they'd made a schedule, ensuring each person had a chance to go at least once in the next week.

It delighted Megan that everyone thought of it as a fun journey, a way of socializing with the town and taking a break from real work. And that's probably why she was looking forward to going. It would give her a chance to reconnect with all of the people she'd known growing up in Bristol Bay.

Lisa was one of her best friends from high school and also the librarian who was allowing them to use the parking lot. It was Chelsea's turn to go today and Dan, the baker, and James, the head chef who made the best truffles. And those were just the ones she knew about.

There were already cars and trucks at Cove House getting the Farm to Fork truck ready to leave. Megan hurried to take a shower and was getting dressed just as she heard a light knock on her bedroom door. Her heart missed a beat, hoping it was Nolan.

"Who's there?" she asked while fluffing her hair. When she didn't get an answer, she opened the door and found New Felicity was waiting patiently in the dark hallway.

"Felicity, what on earth are you doing standing out here in the dark?"

Felicity looked down for a second and then took a deep breath. "I know I'm not on the schedule to go today but I was hoping there was room for me," she told Megan while nervously avoiding eye contact.

Megan wanted to pull her into her bedroom, set her on the bed, and find out everything that was going on in her life. She wanted to smother her with attention and questions and then she remembered what her mother had said about Felicity being secretive. So she simply smiled at

Felicity. "Sure, do you want to ride with me?"

"Are you driving by yourself?" she asked hesitantly.

"No, I was going to go with Nolan and Blake. But you can go with us if you want."

Felicity took a deep breath and her body relaxed. "That sounds fine to me." She backed away from the door and then turned to rush down the hallway. Maybe it was true. Megan was turning into her mother because the more time she spent around Felicity, the more time she was aware of her secretive timid manner. It seems her new glamorous look was only a facade and she was still hiding something.

When Megan walked out of the house, she saw firsthand what getting the truck ready looked like. There was a noisy scurrying of people transferring all of their products to the big green truck and Luke was at the center of it.

Nolan saw her and left Blake to hurry to her. He put his arms around her and whispered in her ear. "Good morning. You're looking especially beautiful today." She giggled and pushed him away. Nolan released her but still kept a hand on her waist.

"Blake loaded part of our stock but there's not enough room for everything. He said we needed to bring more today because they sold out so early yesterday. He's almost finished."

"This looks exciting," she confided in him. "I told Felicity she could ride with us. Have you seen her yet?"

Nolan pointed to his truck. "She's already in there. What's going on?"

"It's just another day of surprises. I have a feeling we don't have to wait long to find out," she hinted.

When they were all settled in the truck, Megan noticed that Felicity had moved a little too close to the middle of the backseat, until she was practically sitting in Blake's lap. They were busy talking and laughing like they were old friends or old lovers. Megan was concerned. There was a fine line between being noticed and being the topic of everyone's gossip.

"Put your seatbelt on, Felicity," Megan told her in a stern voice. It was official. Megan had turned into her mother.

Nolan gave her a worried look. "Safety first," she told him with narrowed eyes.

He tried hard to conceal his chuckling and Megan knew why. She took a quick glance at the backseat again. All of her correcting and mothering had no influence on Felicity or Blake and they seemed oblivious to her piercing stare.

She looked back at Nolan and he shrugged, smiling and shaking his head a little.

"Fine," she said. "I'm done now and officially

resigning my role as her mother." Nolan grinned and held her hand all the way to the library parking lot in Bristol Bay.

FELICITY WAS VERY aware of everything that Megan was doing. She had a plan and her meddling cousin wasn't going to ruin it. Yesterday, after hearing the ladies gossip at Pearls And Curls about Blake, she came up with a plan. The best way to make something true was to submit it to the unofficial news source in Bristol Bay. She was going to give all those ladies something new and exciting to talk about and in the process, she was going to be the only one who had ever tamed Blake Prescott.

She planned to love him and dump him, and in a matter of days, make Luke the most jealous man on the planet. Yesterday, while Howard was helping her with her bags, she caught a glimpse of Luke's face. If he was confused and angry when he watched Howard follow her around, he was going to lose it when he saw her with Blake.

She was right about one thing, Intella-Gwen would most certainly latch on to this tantalizing tidbit. Once it got around town that she was Blake's new girlfriend, other men we're going to take a second look at her. And she would carry this through, upping it more every day, until Luke finally noticed her.

Felicity wasn't worried about hurting Blake's feelings as she was certain he didn't have any. Every family has a ne'er-do-well man who'd never been shot down by a woman. Felicity was looking forward to letting him smell the gunpowder.

She was flirting shamelessly with him, deliberately touching his hand when they talked and subtly running her finger along her bottom lip. A few tilts of her head, a little batting of her eyelashes made his pupils dilate. She'd worn one of her new outfits today and spent a considerable amount of time in front of the mirror with her new top, discovering just how far she needed to lean forward before he'd be able to get a little preview of what she had to offer him.

THE LIBRARY PARKING LOT was already full of people and cars, and much like a carnival, the main attraction was the bright green Farm to Fork truck. It pulled up amid the cheers from the townspeople, many of them back again after trying the locally grown products.

Nolan pulled in close to the truck and started helping Blake unload the surplus cases of beef jerky. But Megan just sat there, overwhelmed and surprised by the staggering greeting from the town. She was grateful for the way everyone in town had pulled together to support the local farmers and appreciated the general feeling of love. She looked around and recognized so many faces. They were friends from school, classmates, and acquaintances, as well as other business owners here to support them.

Nolan opened her door, leaned over her, and unbuckled her seatbelt. "Come on my brave mother hen. It's time for you to protect your little chicken from the big bad wolf out there."

"First, don't ever say those words to me again, and second, you shouldn't assume that Felicity is the one in danger here. Because I'm pretty sure she's got everything under control. I can see that your brother's being squished under her thumb right this very minute."

Nolan looked over at them and saw that Blake was still actively flirting with Felicity. "I'll talk to him but I'm pretty sure he knows better than to start poking around and interfering with your cousins at Cove House."

"Oh, this isn't his first time with the woman at Cove House," she curtly told him. "He was trying with Kate for a while too, coming over and being sweet to her, asking her out and bringing her his beef jerky. I think Kate is pretty taken with him although they never went out on a date. But that doesn't mean there won't be a conflict between Felicity and Kate. We're a family and we'll work it out, whatever Felicity decides."

Nolan reached for her hand. "Come on then, get out of that truck so I can put you smack dab in the middle of the Farm to Fork truck. I want everybody to see the creator behind this project."

"You're terribly funny and it appears that you don't know me at all. I fainted the last time I was the center of something. I hated ballet anyway," she dryly added.

Megan reluctantly jumped out of the truck and into the fire, basking in the heat of it. People she hadn't seen in years came up to her and told her how much they missed her. Her mother's friends were now grandmothers, some of them holding babies in their arms and Megan wistfully remembered having that dream once upon a lifetime ago.

After only two hours, they'd sold all but a few stray heads of purple cauliflower and some artisan lettuce. Megan packed a gift box of their best sellers and wrapped it, putting a little note inside for Lisa. She could have taken it to Lisa herself but she saw something in Dan that made her hope the two of them might be good together.

"I see you sold out again today, Dan. That's so encouraging," she told him while subtly holding the box for Lisa.

He responded with a big smile. "I was up all night baking and now I guess I'm going to do it again. Believe me, I'm not complaining. All of this money is a big help right now."

"You might want to consider opening your own bakery," she told him just as Nolan joined them. "There were so many people who didn't get here before you sold out."

"If you have a few minutes, I'd like to ask a favor," she said as she handed him the box. "A good friend of mine from high school is the librarian here and she's the one who's allowing us to use the parking lot for our sale. I put together a little gift box for her and wondered if you had time to go to the library and find her? Her name is Lisa, she's a wonderful person and if you would, please thank her for all of us. But you have to give it to her, don't leave it for her. It's more personal this way, don't you think?"

A serious look crossed his face. "Of course, I'd be happy to do this for you," he told her.

As Dan hurried off to the Library, Nolan looked at her with narrowed eyes. "What are you up to now?"

"Haven't you ever met someone and instantly known that they'd be perfect for one of your friends?"

"No, and I want to warn you that nothing good ever happens to the matchmaker in that scenario."

"Well. I disagree. He bakes, she loves books; they're perfect for each other."

"If you're so good at this, what makes us perfect for each other?"

Megan audibly sighed. "I don't know yet. Kate said this would happen in two months and so far she's been right about everything. Maybe you should ask her if we're going to last."

He couldn't hide his confidence. "Is she the one who started the rumor that we've been seeing each other?"

"No, darling. It's not a rumor if it's true. Unless you want to disprove it by ignoring me."

"I thought it was to protect your reputation." He tried to smother a laugh but the subtle upward quirk of his mouth gave him away.

"I see. So, is that why you haven't been talking to me or touching me, or even looking at me? You're trying to save me the embarrassment of having you for a boyfriend? And is that because you're old and ugly and disgusting or because you want to remain an eligible bachelor for a while longer?"

"You must have me confused with my younger brother, Blake. I'm not the Casanova of the Prescott family. I'm not going to give Bristol Bay anything to talk about and I'm not putting on a show. A man has to protect the reputation of the woman he loves."

Megan's eyebrows shot up. "And is he planning on telling that woman he loves her? Or is he going to start a rumor and wait until it circles back to her?"

Nolan shook his head, laughing. "I'm pretty sure she already knows. They always say that actions speak louder than words. Maybe I'll show her."

"Look at you and all your threats. It's enough to make any grown woman weak in the knees," she teased him.

"How about when this is all over this morning, I take you back to my place where we can be alone?"

"Sorry, I'm busy today. When we get back to Cove House, everyone's invited to a traditional lobster boil on the beach. And you're included in that if you want to come."

"Is there going to be swimming and bikinis involved in this get-together?"

"Yes darling, you can wear any bikini you like."

Their laughing was interrupted by the unexpected appearance of the original Steel Magnolia.

"Hi, Mom," Megan said. "I didn't expect to see you here."

Alice smiled and pulled her daughter into a hug. "I've missed you, sweetheart. You need to stop by the house when you're in town."

"Did you come down here to shop, Mom? Or to take in the general carnival atmosphere?"

"Neither of those, dear. I brought your father with me." Alice turned and pointed. "He's back there somewhere. Why don't you go find him and bring him here?"

Megan took Nolan's hand and started to take him with her, but Alice stepped in, shaking her head. "If you don't mind, I'd like to have a little chat with Nolan."

Megan waved as she walked away from him. "I'll be back in a minute, Nolan. Don't give up any secrets although I'm certain her bite is worse than her bark. Be careful."

Megan pushed through the crowd, looking everywhere for her dad, finally spotting him standing on a metal folding chair, trying to see over the heads of the people in the crowd. She smiled to herself, realizing that she had a lot more in common with him than she'd ever realized; they were two lost souls looking for a landmark and trying to get home.

Megan waved and called out to him, "Daddy!"

Walter saw his daughter and got off the chair, brushing his hands on his pants as if he'd somehow gotten them dirty. "Come here, Button. Your old dad's missed you."

Megan rushed to hug her dad. "I've missed you so much! You just wouldn't believe everything that's happened to me since I've been back. I can honestly say that I never should have left here and I'm probably the only person who can say they are truly, truly grateful to be divorced and living on a farm in the middle of nowhere. But we have to hurry back. I think Mom's interrogating my boyfriend."

"I heard about him," Walter said as walked with her. "Are you going to keep him?"

"Still testing the waters, Dad. But, yes, so far he's a keeper."

Walter smiled. "I'm happy for you then and I'd like to get to know him if he's going to be part of your life. I already know that your mother approves."

Megan stopped short. "I wouldn't be so sure about that. Look," she said as she pointed to where Alice and Nolan stood facing each other.

Walter hung back. "This doesn't look good, honey. I'm afraid you're going to have to intervene and save him."

Alice kept her voice low and didn't acknowledge their presence. "You can't blame me for wanting to protect Felicity and her reputation. He's old enough to be her father and he needs to tone it down a bit. I can't tell them what they can and can't do but I can certainly make life hard for your family. Acting like this in public is something that could ruin her. You realize that, don't you?

And the poor dear doesn't have a mother or even a father who cares about her, so it all falls to me. I've had so many phone calls this morning, I can't begin to tell you the number of people who are concerned."

Megan waited until her mother finished before voicing her opinion. "Mom, Nolan might be the oldest but I'm pretty sure he can't tell his brother what to do. So you might want to wait and maybe talk to Felicity about it. From what I've seen, she's the aggressor and he's just enjoying the ride. He wouldn't be a man if he didn't. And he's not old enough to be her father."

She looked at Nolan and grinned. "Now, Nolan might be old enough."

He gave her hip a little squeeze and she slapped his hand. Her mother moaned and shook her head. "You're all going to be the death of me."

Megan put her arms around her mother. "Then come to the beach with us and you can have lobster for your last meal. Everyone will be there. Please, Mom."

"I'd love to, Megan. Maybe next time when my nerves aren't all shot to smithereens. Be a good girl. Bye, Nolan. Remember what I said," she told him with her finger in his face.

Nolan was still shaking his head when he put his arm around Megan and pulled her closer than a man should when he had so many onlookers.

"What's with all of the Atwood women sticking fingers in my face because I'm starting to like it."

Megan looked at all the people surrounding them. "You're going to do this right here and right now?"

He nodded and held her tightly in his arms. "I'm officially taking myself off of the market and declaring my love for you and only you, Megan Atwood."

CHAPTER NINETEEN

The living room had been quiet for hours so it was understandable that Megan was somewhat startled when she realized that Kate was standing in front of her. "Did you have fun yesterday?"

Megan looked up from the magazine she was reading. So much happened yesterday and she didn't know exactly what part of it Kate might be referring to. She decided to be safe and remain neutral. "Yes, I meant to compliment you on the lobster boil. I think everyone enjoyed the food and enjoyed the beach. It was a perfect day for swimming, don't you think?"

Kate put her hands on her hips. "Yes, that's what I thought too. But I was talking about something else."

"Of course, watching everybody in town

coming out to support us was wonderful. It's probably the best part about living in Bristol Bay." Megan looked back down and loudly turned another page of the magazine.

"I thought it was great, the day I went. We had so much fun and you were right about the side hustle, we all made a little bit of money."

Megan put her magazine down and sighed. It was her fault for sitting in the open like this. "I haven't asked anybody about the financial side of it and I've wondered if we should keep doing it. Are we making enough of a profit to make it worth the time we put in? Are you as good with numbers as your dad?"

Kate nodded, a serious look on her face. "We don't know how much it cost to turn the tour bus into the Farm to Fork truck, so I haven't been able to factor in those costs yet."

Megan got up from the sofa. "I took care of that part of it because I wanted to do something creative and beneficial for everyone in Bristol Bay. I'm not looking to have the money returned just like I don't want any of the profits. That isn't what's important to me. Besides, that huge tour bus was free. Although, I might've used extortion to get it," she admitted.

"In that case, our numbers are looking great. But we've talked about changing the schedule a little because some of them are having a hard time keeping up with the demand. What do you think about two days a week instead of five?"

"Maybe. I think we were unrealistic when we started, but then we didn't know it was going to be so popular. I'd eventually like to have more trucks and go directly to the farms to pick up what they're selling so everyone doesn't have to come here. I'm kind of drawn to simple, easy things that don't clutter up my day. Rachel is the one who always loved chaos."

Kate looked away and took a deep breath. "Rachel came for the funeral and stayed here for a couple of weeks. Did she come to see you?"

Megan abruptly stood and paced the room, crossing her arms in front of her chest. She knew where this was headed, just like she knew what Kate was going to say next. "How much did she borrow from you, Kate? And don't try to deny it because it's written all over your face." Megan paced a few more steps and stopped. "Oh, please don't tell me she borrowed money from everyone while she was here."

"You know Rachel better than I do and you're right, she borrowed money from all of us. Aunt Alice made her leave when she found out. It was awful," Kate admitted.

"Rachel is sweet and I know it's hard to resist her, but she's family, and I'm going to pay all of you back. If you could just make a list of everything she borrowed and I'll write checks or maybe it's better if I just leave cash for everyone." Megan flopped back down on the sofa, happy that Kate had finally told her what was on her mind.

"Megan, it's not that big of a deal," Kate insisted.

"I grew up with her, remember? Trust me, it's a big deal."

They sat in silence. Megan noticed that Kate was fidgeting and avoiding eye contact with her. "Is there something else, Kate? We spend too much time together to try to hide anything."

"I did have another question but it's not any of my business. It's about Nolan."

Megan stood up and walked to the stairs. "Oh, that's one area that I can't be of any help to you. I do have to tell you that you were right about him and that you should probably start another side hustle telling fortunes. I'm going to go up to my room now and order new clothes. Any suggestions?"

"I'm sure I'll like anything you get as long as it's not stiff like canvas or tan. Pink looks good on me and so does yellow, so keep that in mind if you order tops," Kate suggested.

When Megan got to her room, she pulled out her laptop and tried to do some online shopping but the diary and letters in the attic kept distracting her. She finally gave in and got her skeleton key, unlocking the door bringing everything from that shelf in the bookcase back to her bedroom, and spreading it out on her bed. There were piles upon piles of letters, all wrapped with satin ribbon. The leather-bound diary was bursting full of clippings and foliage, all dried and brittle from being pressed between the pages for one hundred years.

For some reason, she could touch everything but she was having a hard time opening anything. It might be different if these belonged to a stranger, some faceless person from the past without any connection to her.

But the need to know why overcame her. Why was the attic sealed? Why was that piece of furniture put in the attic? Why were all of her letters and her diary kept in there?

The letters were fastened with satin ribbons, each group having a different color of ribbon. They were carefully tied, making it impossible for her to pull out just one letter.

She picked up the pile of letters held together by a red ribbon and carefully untied it. The letters had been crushed together for so long that nothing moved when the pressure of the ribbon was released. She took the first letter off of the pile and examined the envelope. Some of the markings had faded but the handwriting was the same on every envelope. She opened it and pulled out a one-page letter.

My dearest Emma, I feel I must write you again dear altho there is not much news to tell you. Most days I'm asleep on my feet. I tell you it makes a fellow think of lots of things. You'd think I was crazy if I tell you how much I think of you. If only this war was over dear and we were together again. Will close with fondest love and kisses from your Marshall

Megan sat up straight, remembering the name on the crate. This letter was from the same man who sent her the secretary. And this wasn't a letter from a stranger; this letter was from a man that Emma loved. She looked at the date but it had faded and she could barely make out the year, 1917. And then she realized the letter had to have been sent from overseas during the first world war. She rubbed the goosebumps popping up on her arms while knowing full well that they were warning her to stop. She pulled out the second envelope and opened it.

My dearest Emma, I would like to tell you of my love or try to but I know it would be difficult to tell you how much I cared. This day would have been most complete if I could have shared your company for only an hour. Please write back quickly, Your loving Marshall

She felt like an addict. Her brain kept saying,

just one more, just read one more to find out what happened. Before she knew it she'd pulled the third letter from that pile.

My dearest Emma, I received your welcome letters yesterday and it was a little bit of heaven to get your picture. I will keep it close, my love. Now dear Emma I must close but I do so with best wishes for your happiness. May all good come your way. Your loving Marshall

Megan got up from the bed and paced around the room. She knew she'd crossed a line and she could never go back. Violating the privacy of her great grandmother felt worse than she imagined. But she knew one thing for sure; her great grandfather's name was not Marshall. And it sounded like this man loved her and the fact that she kept these letters meant that she loved him too.

Intruding on their love felt like when Kate asked her about Nolan. There wasn't anything to keep secret, it wasn't a forbidden love or even a scandal. They were just normal people in normal times falling in love the normal way with nothing exciting about it. So why couldn't she put everything back in the secretary and leave it alone? It belonged in the past, not on her bed.

She put the letters back in the pile and tied the red ribbon exactly as it had been. And then she took one small peek in the diary. Maybe if she just read the part about why he'd gone to war and why Emma was waiting for him. Or why they were in love, then she'd be able to leave it in the past. It was like starting a story and not knowing how it ended, especially when the end was staring her in the face. She promised herself she would only read the parts that explained why he was writing to her.

She opened up the diary and skipped forward, only reading bits and pieces so that she had some kind of a background to understand Emma. Her maiden name was Sanders and she was born on the land where Cove House stood, overlooking the ocean. She grew up, enjoying the life that her wealthy father provided for her. But he died before she was ten, leaving Emma, her older brother, Michael, and her mother, Margaret. And when Emma was only fifteen years old, she fell in love with Marshall Whitman, a young man from a nearby farm.

By all accounts, it appeared their love was mutual and their commitment for each other was strong so that by the time he left home to serve in the war, she was writing letters to him and waiting for him to come back and marry her.

Megan had her answers and didn't need to continue reading. Her great grandmother had been in love when she was a teenager to a neighbor boy, something common and unremarkable and not the type of thing to be shrouded in mystery. But what did the piece of furniture mean? And why didn't she just burn these letters after she got married? She had to read on to see if Marshall survived the war.

The next part of Emma's diary surprised her. When the war was over, he stayed on, traveling through postwar Europe. What kind of a love story was this? He should have hurried home to her if he loved her.

She picked up the letters and tried to read the dates on the envelopes. The pile with the green ribbon seemed to be the letters from that time. She looked at the outside of the letters and read all of the dates she could make out. He wrote to her persistently and with the reliability of the sun and the moon.

Never a week passed when they didn't correspond with each other. One letter mentioned a pressed tin sweetheart bracelet that he had sent her. Another letter mentioned an engraved gold locket with a rose on it.

Megan tried to stop and found herself picking up one more letter. Perfume from Paris came next, as he traveled through France and on to Italy. From Italy, he sent her cuttings from a vineyard that he proclaimed to have the best wine in the country; those cuttings were followed by even more cuttings and then a case of wine.

Could these be the cuttings that started Bristol Bay Farms Vineyard? Why would he do this for her if he didn't plan on coming back?

She was so overwhelmed that she tied the green ribbon back on the letters as quickly as possible. She took it all back to the attic and put it where it had been, vowing to never look at it again. The more she knew, the more curious she became and realized it might not ever be enough. She might not ever know what happened.

She needed to leave the past behind and concentrate on her now and her future with Nolan. He hadn't promised her anything, but he hadn't left the country either. Only time would tell what would become of their love and their future. And she wasn't anxious to know that either, any more than she wanted to know what had made Emma painstakingly keep everything from a man she never married.

CHAPTER TWENTY

There wasn't a man in Virginia more bewildered than Luke Marshall. He liked to keep his life comfortably diverse, always looking for new projects and new ideas. No one would ever call him stodgy or old-fashioned but the change in Felicity was something he just couldn't understand.

He'd known Felicity since she was in the same kindergarten class with his younger sister, Robin. The girls became best friends and stayed that way, even when Felicity went to live with Coreen Michaelson at Cove House.

In the same way that Coreen had taken Felicity under her wing, she also was there for Luke and his sister. His first job was at Cove house and it was also where he developed his love for the outdoors and caring for animals.

Coreen was very flexible with his schedule.

When he needed time off for school or sports, she always understood without making him feel guilty. And when he was ready to come back to work, his job was always there, waiting for him. In a lot of ways, he thought of Coreen as his grandmother too and her death had devastated him almost as much as it had Felicity.

Maybe it was because he'd been treated like one of the grandchildren that he always saw Felicity as part of his family. And he thought Felicity saw him as a big brother. But lately, she'd been hanging around him more, alluringly moving around the room while talking to him and acting all flustered and nervous. The only way he could handle it was by looking at her as little as possible and trying to think about something else.

Luke was certain that Felicity thought her constant flirting and offers to spend more time with him fell on deaf ears. But his ears were anything but deaf when she was around; he heard every sigh and every word that she uttered. If he looked at her with the same intensity that he listened to her, things would most likely get real awkward real quick.

And now, she'd made it even harder for him. The image of her standing next to the red jeep in her little short dress was something he couldn't get out of his mind. And the thought of Howard hanging around her or possibly touching her was more than he could handle.

Felicity was sweet and vulnerable, always wanting to be helpful and pleasing people. So it wasn't any wonder that the last person he'd ever want to see her with was Blake Prescott. Everybody in town knew about Blake. He was a man who lived on instinct and took any opportunity that came his way without ever considering the consequences. He was older than Luke and undeniably more experienced when it came to women. But when Luke saw Felicity hanging on Blake's arm and blatantly flirting with him, his heart beat a little faster and he unconsciously clenched his fists.

It gnawed at him day and night but he wasn't the kind of person to confront Felicity. It wasn't his place to tell her that she was making a mistake. If her dad had taken any interest at all her, it would have been his responsibility to stop it. And if Grandma Coreen was alive, she would have stopped it the second she saw it happening. But Felicity was alone now and left to drift whichever way the current pulled her.

Until Luke could figure this out, his life was going to be pure suffering and misery. He was the only family Felicity had left and maybe the only person who still cared about what happened to her.

FELICITY WAS SHATTERED by Grandma Coreen's death. It might have been different if she'd seen it coming, not that she'd have ever wished one day of sickness for her grandma. Maybe the suddenness of it is what left her feeling alone and vulnerable, just as she'd felt when she was a child and her mother left her.

Felicity was at college in Charlottesville when she got the simple message from Aunt Alice. Call me back. But Felicity didn't call her or even acknowledge the message. She picked up her purse and got in her car, driving home without ever seeing the road.

There was a hush and emptiness at Cove House when she got there. Her cousins and even Aunt Alice tried to comfort her, but their anxious faces only made the pain sink deeper. She retreated to Grandma Coreen's bedroom and stayed there, avoiding all of the friends and neighbors who came to bring food and express their condolences.

She'd refused to go to the funeral, not wanting to be forced to say goodbye because of a scheduled event. She'd do it when she was ready if she was ever ready. She felt herself shrinking until she was small again, falling back into a black-and-white world.

After the funeral, everything was worse with loud voices, laughing and the sharp sounds of dishes clattering. It didn't make sense. Why was everyone so hungry when she could barely swallow?

She stayed like that for hours, alone except for a single intrusion. When the door opened, her first reaction was that of anger; she hadn't bothered anyone with her grief or asked for special favors. And that's when she saw Luke's subdued face. His arms pulled her into his chest and held her there until she was finally able to cry.

Luke sensed her grief or maybe they were both crushed in the same way. They didn't have the advantage of adult years with adult concerns to dull their childhood memories of Grandma Coreen. And as long as those memories were still alive, Grandma Coreen was alive for them too. It made their common ground rock solid, until the next day when he acted as if it had never happened.

That was the day she moved some of her things into Grandma Coreen's bedroom. She started with her favorite pillow and a blanket, sleeping on top of the bed covers and remembering all the nights she'd spent there listening to Grandma Coreen's stories.

When Felicity came home for Christmas, she began moving her clothes, one rack at a time, into Grandma Coreen's bedroom. She brought down her books and the stuffed animal Luke had given her on her last birthday. She went through her bathroom and pulled everything from body wash to her mascara and put them in a box that she moved last. Now, the only thing left was the window seat and she resigned herself to visiting it.

Felicity was still waiting for someone to tell her that she couldn't stay in Grandma Coreen's bedroom. So she was surprised when she came home after graduation and saw that everything she moved was exactly as she'd left it. It was the biggest bedroom in the house with the largest bathroom and probably the best view of the ocean. It was only a matter of time before Megan asked her to move back upstairs because, by all rights, the master bedroom belonged to her.

And then, there was the dilemma with Blake. He was exhausting to be around, what with having to smile all the time and the pressure to laugh at his stupid jokes. Her back hurt from standing with a perfectly straight spine for hours and hours, smiling at him and trying to stay focused on whatever boring thing that came out of his mouth.

Blake was a cardboard cut-out of a man lacking warmth or humility. The only topic of conversation that interested him was anything that involved himself. He loved talking about cattle and he loved going to restaurants and ordering food. Most of the time, while he rambled on about something that happened to him that day, she was daydreaming about Luke.

It was always Luke, with his beautiful eyes that were a reflection of his beautiful soul. Luke, who was smart and interesting and knew so much about everything. It was always Luke and it was always going to be Luke.

She already wasted so much time before realizing that her normal tactics were never going to get Luke's attention. She was going to have to put her plan in overdrive, hoping for a miracle. And it wasn't as if she wanted all of him. She just wanted him to genuinely look at her and if he would do that she would be the happiest person in the world.

CHAPTER TWENTY-ONE

Bristol Bay's Booming for Freedom Day was one of the town's biggest celebrations of the entire year. Although the Fourth of July was a day of celebration for the entire country, it was especially revered in their historic town, known for having the best festivities in the county. They were so serious about the holiday that it wasn't uncommon for people to greet each other with the words, *"Go fourth in freedom."*

Long before the fireworks were scheduled to start, there would be the annual Independence Parade with flag-draped horses, vintage cars, wagons pulling pets, and the Bristol Bay High School Marching Band.

The Bristol Bay Freedom Run came next but it was only a mile and most people walked while drinking their coffee. The Rotary Club sponsored an old-fashioned Ice Cream & Cake Social during the Little Miss Sparkler Beauty Contest that was held in the town square.

The rest of the day involved homespun family-friendly events: face painting, gunny sack and three-legged races, hula hoop contests, and the vast array of food eating contests. The big events came after the fireworks and after the kids were put to bed. Every year, the adults looked forward to the open-air concerts with local live bands and dancing.

Megan loved all of these activities but the real reason she didn't want to miss the celebration was because of one special booth that sold fat slices of Patriotic Pie; blue and red pies which were technically blueberry and cherry, but they were better than any pies Megan had ever tasted. And that's all she could think about as she rode with Nolan to Bristol Bay. Well, that and his horrible irresponsible brother.

"Why is your brother always such a jerk?" Megan asked while staring out the car window.

Nolan took his eyes off of the road for a second to look at her, curious about what had prompted her question. "I don't know. Maybe it started when he had a tough break up with a girl he'd been with his whole life. And I guess after that, he went through a pretty bad self-destructive phase too. But he might be coming out of it so there's still hope for him. It's even possible that Felicity is good for him. He seems more focused and happy lately."

"So you're saying that dating a younger woman has made him happier? Aren't you talking about every man on the planet?"

"Hey, don't get me confused with Blake. Those girls scared me to death when I was their age and they keep getting more and more scarier the older I get. It's like every new generation is harder to understand."

"Be careful grandpa," Megan admonished him as she tried to stifle a laugh. "I'm pretty sure people have been saying that about young people for thousands of years. You're not the first one to notice."

Nolan smiled to himself. Just when he thought Megan was going to yell at him, she always ended up laughing. He could get used to her humor and also to his new feeling of civic duty. "I hate to tell you this, but this is the first time I've ventured into Bristol Bay for a holiday. It's taken a while, but I'm beginning to feel like part of the town. The people are different from where I came from."

"Well, unless you came from the Moon, I'm pretty sure that all people are the same," she protested. "What makes Bristol Bay different is the sense of community. We take care of each other."

Nolan took a deep breath and glanced

nervously at Megan. "Do you think your parents will be here too? Because I have two requests and I want to ask you about them now before the day gets away from us."

Megan reached over and patted his arm. "Sorry about last time. My dad didn't come over to meet you because he knew what was happening. The reason my parents have had such success in their marriage is that he has the uncanny ability to know when to stay away and keep his mouth shut. I promise that this time, no matter what's happening, I'll introduce you to him. We'd just finished talking about you when we came back and found you having that argument with Mom."

"I didn't even notice your dad was there," Nolan confessed. "Your mom comes on strong and when she got in my face, the only thing I wanted to do was agree with her or do whatever it took to make it stop. And she does it in such a sweet lady-like way so it's hard to even get angry with her."

"I've never heard anyone describe her in that way before. You're an interesting man, Nolan Prescott."

Nolan smiled a little. "You take after her. Like the time in the barn when you were scolding me, poking your finger in my face and all I could think about was the tiny little thing you were wearing and how every time you moved it slipped around. And there I was, trying so hard to keep my eyes on your face and not look down. It was a hell of a morning on all accounts."

"You like remembering that, don't you? How long had you been sequestered on that ranch?" she teased him.

"I don't know but let's get back to the two things I wanted you to promise. One of them wasn't meeting your dad but I'd like that and it's not about your mother either. She's growing on me. It's weird but I understand where she's coming from."

"Okay, I'll bite. What are the two things?" Megan prodded.

"They're both things that happen later in the day. I'd like to dance with you and go someplace where we could be alone to watch the fireworks. I brought a blanket in the truck. Maybe for once, we could be like normal people and not the couple everyone's watching."

"That's so romantic and sweet, Nolan. But have you ever been to one of these town fireworks displays before?"

"No, when we were growing up, we always set off our fireworks in our yard. Why?"

Megan regarded him with amusement. "I want to explain this without panicking you, but the way it works, every inch of the ground will be covered with people. There won't be a private spot and if we're lucky, we won't go home with someone else's children. The kids tend to wander around."

"Oh. I'm a little disappointed but I understand," he admitted.

They reached Bristol Bay early enough in the day to find a good parking spot and Megan dragged him directly to the Patriotic Pie booth. "This is always my first stop because if you wait until night, all the pie is gone. We have to get a slice of blueberry and cherry unless you want to have your own."

The line was short and they were to the front and no time. Megan took the cherry and Nolan took the blueberry and they decided to eat standing up.

Nolan watched as Megan cut a little piece of both pies and put both of them on her fork. Her eyes immediately teared up and her mouth puckered. "This has to be just the best pie in the world. I don't know why people don't bake them this way on purpose. I'd call it bluecherry pie."

Nolan did the same thing but with different results. He sputtered, his face turning red before finally swallowing it. "This tastes an awful lot like a bitter sweet-tart which means it's double tart and only a little sweet. How can you eat this?"

"Come on, Nolan," Megan protested. "I haven't had Patriotic Pie in years so don't ruin it for me."

"Maybe I'll wait and get something to eat later. I'll just stand here and watch your eyes water," he said while wrinkling his nose. "Worst pie I've ever tasted."

Megan answered by taking another bite. "I guess I get to eat all of it then, right?"

Nolan looked past her and Megan turned just in time to see Lisa running toward her. "Look who's here! My best friend who disappeared in New York City. I've missed you, Megan," Lisa told her while giving her a big hug.

Megan tried to wipe the cherry and blueberry juice from her face while using her other hand to hold the pie. "Well, life moves faster in the city and I felt like I was only there for seconds. But you haven't changed one bit, Lisa. You're still the prettiest girl at Bristol Bay High."

Lisa blushed and covered her face with her hand. "You were always the biggest flirt, handing out compliments like candy and you're still doing it. Thank you so much for all of the fun boxes you've been giving me, although I think that you're secretly just trying to make me fat."

"Are you talking about the box I sent last week?" Megan asked. "I sent you mainly healthy things, like eggs and honey. Remember?"

A look of confusion crossed Lisa's face. "Is this some kind of a joke? Because you've been sending me a box every day for the last week. Ask Dan, he'll tell you."

Megan was perplexed. "Now I feel horrible,

Lisa. I only sent you one box and if you got more, they were from Dan, not me. By chance, were the boxes filled with the most wonderful bakery goodies you've ever had in your entire life?"

Lisa silently nodded, her face dazed. "Wonderful pastries and the best bread. Dear Lord, he's seducing me with whoopie pies and cannoli."

"And it's working," Megan noted. "As long as we're on the topic of wonderful men, I'd like you to meet my boyfriend, Nolan Prescott. And Nolan, this is Lisa Evans, my best friend in the whole world. We were inseparable."

"We had the best times," Lisa sighed. "Sometimes I wish I could go back to those days."

"Lisa, our best times are ahead of us. Now, tell me about Dan. He was the real reason that I sent you the box," Megan confided in her.

"Dan's wonderful. Smart and witty. But, I thought he was just being polite and helping you. Does he know you were trying to set us up?"

"No. That would have made him uncomfortable and I wanted you to see the sweet genuinely good side of him first before he had to do all the awkward stuff."

"Awkward stuff?" Lisa asked.

"Yes, awkward, Lisa. Don't you remember high school? I watched while confident boys turned into blubbering idiots the second you said hi to them. I didn't want that to happen to Dan so I gave him a task, a favor. He was shielded by that and it took away the awkwardness. But it turns out he didn't need any help after all. Just a little push in your direction."

"Stop it," Lisa admonished her. "He's not interested in me. He was just being nice."

"I think the whoopie pies are telling you something different than nice. He made his move, now it's your turn. Invite him for a home-cooked dinner," Megan advised her.

Lisa laughed. "You're right. We're just talking away and there you are, Nolan. Being so polite and not acting bored with our conversation. What a gentleman."

Nolan smiled at her compliment. "I only have brothers so I've never heard this side of the conversation before. I thought that only men second-guessed everything. This is eye-opening, to say the least."

Megan put her arm in his and smiled up at him. "We should get some real food. Would you like to join us, Lisa?"

"I'd love to but I'm just on my way to pick up my mom. We'll be back before the fireworks start."

"Okay. See you later and save some of those whoopie pies for me!"

They got two steps away from Lisa and Nolan laughed. Megan stuck her finger in his face with a warning. "Don't even start with the whoopie comments. I could hear you snickering and prayed you'd hold it in."

"Hold what in, dear?" Alice came out of nowhere and Megan considered that her mother had installed a tracking device in her tooth when she was a teenager. She'd threatened both of her girls, telling them dentists could install them under the guise of removing a tiny bit of decay. A miniature solar battery could power it for a lifetime. She hadn't opened her mouth when she was outside for years after that.

"Nothing, Mom. Nolan likes it when I point my finger in his face. Tell her why you like it so much, Nolan," she told him while playfully poking his arm.

"Oh, Megan. Leave that poor boy alone. It's entirely possible to tease a person to death, you know. Martha Edwards had that happen to her great aunt."

"Where's Dad?" Megan asked. "You didn't lose him again, did you?"

Alice looked around at the crowd and took a big breath. "He's here somewhere. He was talking to someone about a tree. I mean, who'd actually sue their neighbor over a tree? It's ridiculous if you ask me."

Megan searched the crowd for any sign of him. Her dad was always getting stopped at events like this and he never hesitated to give out free advice.

"That's odd," Megan told them. "While I was looking for Dad, I noticed that Kate's here. I just saw her over there, standing next to the snow cone stand. She told me she had too much to do today and wouldn't be coming for the fireworks."

"It looks like she's babysitting those two adorable children. I didn't know she was working two jobs. Where could the parents be on a holiday that they couldn't take their children? I certainly hope there hasn't been an emergency," Alice worriedly told them.

"I'm sure it's nothing, Mom. I probably shouldn't have even brought it up. I've been concerned because she's always so tired but she's never mentioned a babysitting job and we've spent a lot of time talking about side hustles."

Alice's eyes widened. "Why didn't you tell me she was that desperate for money? I hope it's nothing illegal. The thought of that child having to hustle people to cover her expenses turns my blood cold."

Megan shook her head. "It's not that kind of hustling and she's not doing anything illegal. I thought we were beginning to be friends so I'm sure there's a good reason why she changed her mind about coming today. We should just forget about it and find Dad. The fireworks are almost ready to start and I hoped we could all sit together," Megan told her mother while smiling at

Nolan.

He made a sad face. She bopped him on his nose. He feigned pain and she kissed his nose. He tickled her and her legs gave out, crying with laughter. He caught her before she fell to the ground.

Alice sighed loudly. "I'm getting Walter and we'll find a good place to sit. In the meantime, neither of you is allowed to move or tease each other. It's like you're twelve again," she muttered under her breath.

CHAPTER TWENTY-TWO

Felicity's first memory of the Fourth of July was when she was three years old. Her parents took her to watch the fireworks and were dismayed to discover that she hated the noise, she hated the dark, she hated all the people. They put her back in the car, maneuvered out of the parking lot, and took her home.

Her next memory of the Bristol Bay Booming For Freedom Day was with Grandma Coreen. They spent the day eating cotton candy and snowcones and Grandma Coreen entered her in the Little Miss Sparkler Beauty Contest. With nothing more than a sparkly leotard and tap shoes, she sang and danced her way to first prize and still has the little rhinestone crown proudly displayed on her bedroom dresser. Since then, the Fourth of July has been her favorite holiday.

When Robin called her and asked that they spend the day together, Felicity jumped at the opportunity. She'd missed seeing Robin but understood that Robin's full-time job was a priority. It made this day their own special freedom day.

They decided to bypass all the little kid activities and instead waited until after dark to squeeze their way through the crowds of families to watch the sky being set ablaze with the glowing colors of patriotism. There was nothing as spectacular as fireworks being set off over the ocean, transforming their bay into a glowing rainbow of dazzling prisms of colored light, repeatedly shocking everyone with pyrotechnic precision.

When the last boom was over, they held hands and headed straight for the large tents, knowing the music was going to be starting.

"The fireworks were amazing, as usual," Robin told her. "But I'm anxious to see what bands are playing this year."

"I've been so busy lately that I haven't had a chance to check," Felicity confided in her. "But if it's anything like last year, it's going to be fantastic."

It turned out they weren't the only ones headed straight for the area set aside for the open-air concerts. They came around the corner just in time to see Blake and Teddy walking with some of their friends.

Robin made a dead stop and grabbed Felicity's arm. "Isn't that your boyfriend, Blake Prescott? I know you haven't exactly told me he's your boyfriend but according to the Bristol Bay Rumor Mill, you guys are hot and heavy right now. How'd you swing that?"

Felicity tossed her hair and pointed to the crowd of young girls walking toward Blake and his group of friends. The girls were all dressed in short skirts and cowboy boots and looking for trouble. But Blake didn't seem to notice, locking eyes with Felicity and smiling.

"That's how I do it," she proudly announced. "He hasn't been able to look at another woman since he met me. I do think he's fallen madly in love with me. Sadly, I'm not ready to settle down so he'll just have to wait for me."

Robin looked at her with surprise. "Where's my best friend? I don't know if it's your new blonde hair or your new clothes but you've changed. I'm starting to feel sorry for Blake, even though I'm sure there are plenty of women who think he has it coming to him."

When Felicity and Robin reached Blake and his group of friends, Blake went straight to Felicity picking her up and making a big show of twirling her before setting her back down. He ended the performance with a hard kiss smack on her lips.

It was unclear if Felicity was writhing pleasure or simply trying to escape his grasp and his mouth. When he finally let her come up for air she stood back and looked at him with surprise. "What? I mean, what's gotten into you?"

Blake winked at her and smiled so wide she could see his tonsils. "Just happy to see ya, darlin'. How about we find someplace quiet and have a few drinks before we start dancing?"

Felicity glanced over her shoulder at Robin who appeared to have already agreed with Blake. "It's fine with me but you have to remember that I don't get to spend much time with Robin. Anything we do has to include her."

Blake rested his arm on Felicity's shoulder while simultaneously winking at Robin. "You let me worry about that. I'm going to take good care of both of you."

They walked as a group, passing several bands before Robin suddenly grabbed Felicity's arm and shook it with excitement. "This is Luke's band. The one I told you about, remember? I've heard them before and they're so good! We have to stay for a while."

Felicity's mouth fell open in shock. "What?"

Robin was surprised by her reaction. "Wait. Maybe I told someone else. But you already knew that Luke's been playing the guitar forever. And now he's joined up with some of his friends, people he knew from high school and college, and they put together this little band. First, it was just something they did to mess around but lately, they've gotten popular. He didn't tell you?"

Felicity was stunned. She was already at a disadvantage and now she had more competition than she could count. The sharp weight of it made her stomach sick.

"Gee, Robin. I guess it must be something that just slipped your mind. Did anything else slip your mind? Like you got married or you're going to climb Mount Everest? Because this is a big thing and I can't believe you didn't tell me. But most of all, I see him every day and he didn't even mention it. I guess I'm not that important for anybody to even think of me at all."

Robin shushed her and pushed her into a chair, motioning to Blake and his friends. "Let's all stay here and listen to my brother's band."

Teddy started to sit down but Blake's eyes went black as he looked directly at Robin. "Maybe later. I think Felicity and I will go on to the next band."

Blake tugged at Felicity's shoulder but she waved him off and smiled. "Blake, give me a little kiss and I'll be over to meet you in a few minutes. Robin asked me to stay with her while her brother plays. Okay? Bye-bye, see you later, honey."

Blake wasn't used to being dismissed in this

manner but he took it like a gentleman, pulling her out of her chair and giving her a big kiss before depositing her back in the chair. He wiped his mouth with his sleeve and glared at Luke.

Robin chuckled under her breath and whispered in Felicity's ear. "If he was a monkey, he'd be throwing stuff at Luke right now. But men are so stupid, aren't they? Can you believe he thinks Luke is his competition? That's the funniest thing I ever heard."

Felicity nodded, trying not to breathe or move. She wanted Blake to leave just like she wanted to wipe her mouth, but Luke was still staring at her so she smiled and pretended like nothing out of the ordinary had happened.

The drummer started with a few beats and Luke got up from the table, leaving his adoring groupies. Blake offered his hand, giving Felicity one last chance to leave with him. But she ignored him and he reluctantly left with his friends.

Felicity counted four people; one on drums, one on the keyboard, one violinist, and Luke on the guitar. She sighed in relief until she saw a young woman climb on stage next to Luke. She had bleached white-blonde hair and the kind of curves that could only be bought. Could things get any worse?

Felicity elbowed Robin. "What kind of music do they play? And what's with that woman? She looks too old to sing with a country band."

"They play Country Rock and her name's Georgia. She's super nice and went to college with Luke so she can't be that old," Robin told her.

"Maybe I should change my name to Pennsylvania. The girls with the fun names seem to get all the attention," Felicity muttered.

The first set was flawless but Felicity couldn't hear the music because she was so intent on watching Luke. Luke playing the guitar. Luke smiling. Luke with that woman and all her fringe and dazzling flash.

Robin ordered drinks and the waiter kept delivering them but Felicity was unable to swallow. Her drinks piled up until Robin drank them for her. By the time the set was over, Robin was a bit wobbly and a bit smeared with lipstick.

"Come on, I think we need to get you home," Felicity told her. "It's getting late."

"I don't know what you're talking about," Robin insisted. "I'm fine, I just need to get up and move and maybe get some air. We need to dance. Come on Felicity, let's go dance."

Luke put his beer on their table, leaning toward them and smiled. "Did you like our first set? We're playing again in a few minutes. Can you stay a little longer?"

"That's nice and maybe if your sister can sober up, we might consider staying. Who are those girls?" Felicity asked, slightly stuttering.

Luke took off his hat and carefully placed it on the table, stalling for more time. "Just some of my friends who always show up when we play."

Felicity smiled sweetly and cocked her head. "Friends, like the people who bring you soup when you're sick? Or the kind of friends that'll get in bed with you to keep you warm when you're sick?"

Luke lowered his eyes, noticeably blushing. He never should have looked directly at Felicity because that familiar tightening was starting in his chest. "Well, if those are your definitions of friends, I guess we're more friendly than actual friends. I don't know anyone who would even bring me soup much less warm my bed."

He picked up his beer and leaned toward his sister. "You need to come out to Cove house and visit me sometime, Robin. Things have been a little quiet without Grandma Coreen. I wish I could see you more often."

Luke grabbed his hat from the table and stuck it back on his head, casually walking to where a table of young women was smiling at him.

"What's up with him?" Robin muttered.

"I'm sure I wouldn't know. Seems like he has his hands full, what with all those women clamoring for him and jumping up and down like they're giggling preteen fans," Felicity retorted.

Robin looked at her curiously. "What's gotten

into you? I think both of you have the same problem and no one's bothering to tell me. I thought this was going to be a fun night, not an evening of bickering."

Felicity looked down at her hands and nodded. "I'm sorry, Robin. I'd like to blame it all on Grandma Coreen but I think it's more than that. I'm just so sad all the time and every time I'm around Luke he's impatient or angry. Maybe both of you would be better off without me."

Robin's eyes widened and she sucked in a quick breath. "I didn't mean that the way it sounded, Felicity. Honest. And the last thing I want is to see less of you. I feel a little lost too. At least you and Luke are together at Cove House and can always lean on each other."

Felicity sadly shook her head. "It's not like that. I barely see Luke and he never talks to me. I'm completely alone. At least you have your parents."

"It might seem like that," Robin admitted. "But Mom and dad are always working. Mom had to take on extra shifts to support me through school. You don't know how lucky you are. Grandma Coreen always took such good care of you and I'm pretty sure that you have enough money in your inheritance to pay for school and anything else you want."

Felicity nodded and chewed on her lower lip.

"You're right. You're right about everything. I don't have to worry about paying back school loans. I don't even have to worry about how I'm going to pay my phone bill because Grandma Coreen made sure that would never happen to me. But do you know all the things money can't buy? Because I do and if you want to hear about that I'd be happy to tell you anytime you want."

There was a long silence. "When you say it like that, it makes me sound like a selfish monster. I'm sorry I said anything. It's the drinks," Robin admitted.

Felicity was anxious to change the subject. "Maybe I should text Blake and tell him that we're ready to party with him and his friends. I feel like we need to spend just one night not worrying about our problems. What do you think?"

Robin gave her a sheepish look. "You know that I have a boyfriend but I wouldn't mind having some cute looking guy try to distract me for a little while. So go ahead, tell him where we are and see if he'll come back and get us."

Felicity pulled out her phone and then nodded at Robin. "Done and done. Now, all we have to do is wait."

But they didn't have to wait very long. Blake showed up, slightly intoxicated, with three of his best buddies in tow. They bowed, took off their hats, and smiled at the two girls. Robin and

Felicity looked at each other and then smiled back at them.

Felicity leaned closer to Robin. "I'll be leaving with Blake and you get to choose between the other three boys. Make them fight for you," she added.

She stood up and took one last look at Luke. He was still sitting at the table with all those women congregated around him. But he was stone-faced and openly staring at her. She was surprised and a little flattered. He wasn't even trying to hide his piercing glare. He looked jealous.

Blake put his arm around her and they moved out of the tent and on to the next live band. She got a chance to look over her shoulder one last time and met Luke's eyes. Her heart pounded when she realized that this wasn't going to be the end for them.

And that was a promise that was written all over his face.

CHAPTER TWENTY-THREE

*K*ate was getting used to seeing Nolan every morning, but there were times she wished he would just bring his clothes over and move in. Then he would be more of a resident and less of a guest and she wouldn't have to keep smiling whenever she saw him.

If he was anything like Blake, he would soon tire of Megan and leave her heartbroken and confused. Kate worried about Megan and how quickly she'd jumped into this relationship without knowing anything about the Prescotts.

Blake had done the same thing to her. He came to Cove House at least once every day to see her. He brought her flowers and candy, sweet gifts that were a cliche' for most people, but she loved them. He was quick with compliments and had that heart-thumping smile that always worked for him. It worked for her as well, something she was sorry to admit. And she fell for him almost as fast as Megan fell for Nolan. Kate learned the hard way and wanted to spare Megan from the inevitable heartache that was sure to come.

Breakfast was ready. The crispy bacon was fresh from the frying pan and the hotcakes were warming in the oven. For some reason, Megan always wanted to send Nolan off in the morning with coffee and a breakfast that she never actually made. Kate knew it was her bad mood and jealousy that prompted these thoughts. After all, her job was to do the cooking. She couldn't handpick who she wanted to serve. Lately, having one of those Prescott brothers at her table was just a little too much for her to stand.

Megan and Nolan were making a racket on the stairs like they did every morning. In fact, they made a racket wherever they went, always laughing and teasing, their happiness shining on their faces like a neon light. A neon light that cut tiny slices in Kate's heart and made her lungs shrink every time she saw them.

"Morning, Kate," Megan told her as she snatched a piece of bacon from the plate. "I'm going to grab some food so we can sit on the veranda and watch the sunrise over the ocean."

Kate didn't look up at her and simply shrugged. "Sure. I'll grab a couple of cups of coffee for you and bring the napkins and silverware out to you in a minute."

Megan's face fell. "Aren't you going to eat with us? I'm sure the men have already been through here and Felicity will probably sleep until tomorrow. Why don't the three of us have breakfast together?"

A wave of guilt swept over Kate. It wasn't Megan's fault or even Nolan's fault that Blake had decided he liked the youngest of the female cousins at Cove House. And it wasn't their fault that Felicity had made herself so blatantly available to Blake, all the while knowing that Kate had feelings for him too. Not all of her cousins were backstabbing thieves, just the last one she'd have ever suspected.

"I'm not that hungry but I could use another cup of coffee. Are you sure I won't be interrupting?"

"Don't be silly, Kate. And if I ever make you feel like you're interrupting us, I want you to call it to my attention. This probably won't last forever anyway."

Kate spun around to face Megan. "What are you talking about? I told you from the beginning that the two of you were perfect together and I was right. I feel like you're trying to put a hex on it or something."

Megan relaxed against the wall and

contemplated Kate's reaction. "It's not a hex but more like acceptance. If I hang onto him too tightly, I'll strangle the life out of him. So I have to accept that he'll either go or stay and hope he stays."

Kate furrowed her brow. "What's wrong with you? You were so happy five minutes ago."

"Yes, and I'm happy now but I'm not ever going to take Nolan for granted. Haven't you ever been scared and happy at the same time? Like when something seems so wonderful that your heart will burst, but at the same time you worry it's all going to be lost?"

Kate nodded. "I've felt like that every day for quite a while now. But it doesn't have anything to do with a man."

"So, what's it about then? What are you afraid of losing, Kate? If you tell me, maybe I can help you." Megan pleaded.

Kate quickly moved away from Megan as if she'd just remembered something important. "I don't know why I'm feeling so dramatic today. With Felicity in her room all the time and you with Nolan, sometimes I feel alone out here."

"I've been thinking the same thing. How about asking Chelsea to come here for the rest of the summer?" Megan suggested. "We have so much fun when all of us are together."

Kate nodded. "Like that day when Steve was here. It was fun and then horrible and then we had a party and it was fun again. Do you think that there's something wrong with our family? Is that even normal?"

Megan shrugged. "Who knows what's normal? That's why we need Chelsea here. She'll be the person to balance everything out. And we have so many extra bedrooms if she wants to stay. How about you? Will you move in here too? Oh, please. It would mean so much to me."

Kate pulled out a tray from the buffet and put the plates of food on it. She added silverware and napkins and then the cups of coffee before handing it to Megan. "I can't, Megan. I have a lease and other responsibilities. But I guess it wouldn't hurt to ask Chelsea if she wants to spend some time here with us, would it?"

Megan took the tray from her and nodded towards the door. "If you could get the door, I'll take this out, and right after breakfast, I'll call Chelsea. I love you and I'll do anything I can to make you happy, Kate. I can't do anything about Felicity and Blake, but I'll do anything else if it will make things easier for you."

Kate smiled at her and opened the door for her. "Thanks, Megan. I love you too."

NOLAN HUNG AROUND after breakfast helping Megan by taking their plates back to the kitchen and then following her back upstairs.

Megan eyed him curiously. "Are you taking the day off? Or just the rest of the morning?"

Nolan grinned, looking more mischievous than normal. "I want to show you something but we need to go on horseback. I just need to saddle a couple of horses for us."

"When did you become so mysterious?" she asked. "This isn't going to be a Hansel and Gretel situation, is it? Because sometimes you look at me like you could devour me in one bite."

Nolan laughed and shook his head. "I think you're getting your fairy tales mixed up. You're talking about the little girl with the red cape aren't you?"

"I never thought about it before but I guess they all end the same way, don't they?   But sure, I'd love to go for a ride with you," she told him. "Just let me change into something other than shorts. I'm not venturing away from the house ever again without the proper clothes."

Megan changed into jeans and boots and they left through the front door. She took Nolan's hand and squeezed it. "If Luke's in the barn, maybe we could settle the arrangements for Elsa's mother?"

Nolan shrugged. "Luke is efficient. He settled all that months ago. It seems you had your heart set on owning that cow, right?"

"I know it makes me sound corny and soft-hearted but I couldn't bear separating them and the thought that they'd never see each other again was unbearable. That and I'd already named her Betsy."

Nolan put his arm around her shoulders. "That's one of the things I love about you. You're so sentimental when it comes to animals. But you wouldn't be the first person to have a cow for a pet."

"Really? I've never had a pet other than a hamster, and that was when I was a child. So I guess I started small and ended big. How long do cows live, anyway?"

"Twenty-three years or more and I suspect longer since you have a good vet on call."

Megan observed him thoughtfully. "I'm impressed that you know all that. I won't be needing to get another pet for a very long time."

Luke was in the barn, busy moving hay and feeding the horses. "It looks like you plan on taking a ride. How many horses do you want me to saddle?"

Nolan held up two fingers and looked around the barn. "Where's Jeff? Megan said that he was taking care of the horses now."

Luke was already busy getting the horses when Jeff joined him. He smiled at Megan while lifting the saddle onto her horse. "Do you know where you're going today? Because I have strict orders to always accompany you. I could trail along behind if you like."

Nolan turned to Megan and shook his head a little. "What's all this?" he asked her in a low voice.

She patted his arm. "My mom can't be here to make sure I'm safe so Jeff was hired to ride with me. He's just trying to do his job, Nolan."

Megan went over to pet her horse. "Thank you for your concern, Jeff, but Nolan and I will be fine on our own."

Jeff nodded and gave her the reins. "Yes, ma'am. I completely understand."

THEY RODE OUT into the endless sea of green, flower and fern still slick with the morning dew. Purple coneflowers dribbled out from the tree line and filled the meadows as they raced past. They only slowed when the horses had to pick their way through the pathless forest, dangerous with the uneven ground and gnarled roots underfoot.

"I used to love the forest when I was a child, the way it's so quiet and dark. The wind doesn't even make a sound," Megan whispered as they moved slowly in single file.

"They let you ride out here by yourself?"

"Sometimes. My grandma usually came with

me. She had a favorite spot out here where her mother used to have picnics with her. She did the same for me. We had picnics in the forest and picked white fairy candles to be the centerpiece."

"Fairy candles?"

"Those white flowers over there." She pointed to the white spindles rising from the ground. "They only bloom in the woods. And don't ever confuse them with Poison Hemlock. They're white flowers too but they look like little umbrellas. They're not as poisonous as Spotted Water Hemlock though. Now that I think about it, it's probably best to never touch a plant with white flowers."

"Good to know," Nolan said. "And white seems like such an innocent color."

"I know. But you'd be wrong. All of this seems like common knowledge to me so I forget that it's something you learn from your parents or, in my case, my grandma. My ancestors settled in Jamestown in 1607, years before the Mayflower ever set sail. That's over four hundred years, sixteen generations, and a lot of acquired knowledge about Virginia. But it's boring now that I hear myself talking."

They made it through the narrow forest and came out into the open again. They took off, flying through the stretch of meadows until Nolan slowed again. Their horses walked side by side, lulling them.

"You've never said anything about your family, Nolan. Where are you from?"

"We moved here from Birmingham. My grandfather immigrated when he was a young man, so I don't have a long lineage like you. It's never been important for us to trace our ancestors." Nolan felt guilty about lying to her but it was just a half-lie. They'd worked the pipelines in Birmingham to make money to buy their land but he was born here in Virginia, not far from Bristol Bay.

"Is there an interesting story behind why you decided to come here?"

"We came here because Virginia has the flattest land and the biggest sky I've ever seen. And we've never met more neighborly people than we have here. I'd like to own more land someday and probably have more cattle. How about you? What are your plans?"

"I thought I wanted to travel but now that I'm here, I don't want to leave. I'd like to get another food truck and start a camp for kids. And I'd like to start remembering my dreams again. I used to have so many dream adventures that spilled into my awake life too. I haven't had a dream in, well, forever."

Nolan smiled and shook his head. Sometimes he felt like she was a translucent butterfly, too fragile to touch. It was a miracle that they could exist together, their differences were so great. Maybe that's what made them perfect for each other. "Everyone has dreams, Megan. Why don't you just decide to remember them?"

"That's an excellent idea. I'll do it tonight. If you're there when I go to sleep, will you remind me?"

"Where else would I be?" He chuckled with amusement.

"You said you had something to show me."

"Right up here," he pointed as the horses slowed to a halt. There was a break in the fence, wide enough for two horses to pass through at the same time. The sides were finished and a wood trellis arching high over the opening.

"What is it, other than a break in the fence?" she murmured.

"It's a shortcut between our houses. I calculated a straight line, the fastest way for us to reach each other, and made sure you could find it from a distance. I'm going to plant flowering vines to grow over it. I heard what you told Kate before breakfast, so I wanted to show you this."

"Kate and I talked about quite a few things this morning, mainly about her sad mood lately. If you were listening, then you know it's because of Blake."

"I wasn't eavesdropping," he insisted. "The

window was open and I was sitting right there. It's as if you wanted me to hear your conversation with Kate."

"Of course not. But I called Chelsea and it's been settled. She's moving to Cove house today. Chelsea and Kate are close and Kate needs someone right now. Maybe her mood will improve."

"Yes," he told her impatiently, "but it's what you said about us being temporary. You told her that everything ends. I can promise you that we're not going to end but then I thought if I showed you this first, you'd see that I'm planning a future with you. Someday, someone who never knew us will find this and wonder why anyone would put so much work into keeping a fence open."

All of this was eerily similar to the mystery surrounding Emma and Marshall. She wasn't going to end up like Emma, loving a man she couldn't have and then hiding the evidence of it. She tried to stop the words but the truth of them got the best of her.

"And will it be a lost secret because we never married? Or because any link between us will be lost and covered by weeds? Because that sounds like the opposite of romantic. It's a sad story with a bitter end and I don't want any part of it."

Nolan was surprised by her outburst. "Is that what you want? Because it's what I want too. We can get married today. I'm not leaving you, no matter how much you push me away."

Megan sucked in a sharp breath. "You'd do that? Are you crazy? We can't get married today. My mother would have a fit and my dad would never forgive me. Maybe we should talk about this tomorrow when I'm not so upset about Kate."

"I know you're worried about Kate but she's better off without Blake," he insisted. "You should be more worried about Felicity,"

Megan sighed and looked back at the arbor. "I'm not convinced that she feels anything for Blake but I could be wrong. And the arbor is beautiful, almost as beautiful as the thought behind it. Just promise me you won't ever let it get overgrown with weeds."

CHAPTER TWENTY-FOUR

*M*egan and Nolan arrived back at Cove House at the same time as Chelsea pulled up in her overstuffed car. Nolan took both horses back to the barn so that Megan could greet her cousin.

"I hope this wasn't inconvenient, having to pack all of your things to move on such short notice. Do you want me to get Luke to help with the heavier things?"

Chelsea gave her a big smile and threw her arms around her. "You don't have any idea how much I've wanted to live here with all of you."

Megan hugged her back and smiled in agreement. "We should've done this a long time ago. Did they mind when you moved out of Jameson House?"

Chelsea shook her head. "No, I had an

apartment in Bristol Bay but I was living alone and hated it. Luckily, I was at the end of my lease. I sure won't miss all my noisy neighbors."

Megan chuckled. "You're taking a chance because you might discover that we're noisy too. Try to remember how much you love us when we're keeping you up all night."

"Are you kidding? I'll be the one leading the party," she said with a sly smile.

Megan motioned to the barn. "I'm going to get Nolan and find out who else is in the barn. I'll get someone to take all of your things to your bedroom. Why don't you go to the house and find Kate? I know she's been anxious to see you."

When Megan entered the barn, the men were talking about horses and feed and how the new calf was doing. Megan had to interrupt. "Are there any volunteers to help Chelsea move her bags to her bedroom? We would do it except that we're going to start dinner now."

Howard and Jeff started for the house and Megan motioned for Nolan to follow her. Once they were out of earshot from the others, she kissed him and whispered in his ear. "We have a full house now. Do you want to come and help me move some boxes in my room while everyone else is busy making dinner?"

Nolan nodded and they went hand in hand into the house, making a stop in the kitchen to get water after their long ride. As Megan stood at the kitchen sink, she was reminded of a time not so long ago when she'd done this exact thing. She'd stared out of her kitchen window, alone and in the cold darkness, facing a bleak future.

The dead soil had been replaced with the fertile green lushness of pastures and forests. The emerald blue water of the ocean had washed over her, freeing her from that barren life. She felt alive and enthusiastic about every new day.

Nolan came from behind her and wrapped his arms around her. "What has you so deep in thought?"

"I was just thinking about how life is surprising. I never thought I'd be here or with you. Two months ago, I was ready to leave everything behind and travel alone. I'd forgotten that I had a family. I'd forgotten who I was. All of this made me remember and I'm more thankful than I could have ever imagined."

Nolan nodded and buried his face in the side of her neck. He kissed down her neck and onto her shoulder. "I know exactly what you mean. I don't even remember the man I was before I met you. I was angry about things that don't even matter to me anymore. I can't believe I wasted so much energy on trying to get somewhere else, thinking I'd be happier. Then you happened, a contradictory ball of love and fury. It's going to take the rest of my life to try and figure you out."

Megan laughed. "Well, I hope you're not too disappointed when you find out that I'm very basic, with no secrets or surprises. Being out on the land today was peaceful and a nice way to start the day. We should do it more often, don't you think?"

He nuzzled her neck again until she turned to kiss him. Their eyes were dreamy and they were alone with their love until the kitchen door flew open and Felicity rushed in.

"I've had the best day," she gushed. "And I bet you'll never guess where I've been."

Megan took one look at her and immediately knew where she'd been but didn't dare ruin Felicity's moment. "I couldn't guess although you look especially beautiful today."

Kate joined them in the kitchen and glared at Felicity. "What have you done now? Are you going through a quarter-life crisis?"

Felicity smiled at them, ignoring Kate. "I just came from Pearls and Curls and they hired the most amazing girl. She's beautiful with the darkest hair and eyes. She put extensions on my eyelashes and I'll never need to wear mascara again."

"So that's what's different. I see it now," Megan told her with an approving tilt of her head. "Your skin looks amazing too. Did you have a facial?"

"Oh, more than a facial," Felicity confided. "It was this whole process with retinoids and oils and masks. It took hours but was so worth it. She's an esthetician, all the way from Richmond, and her schedule is already full for the next month. I was lucky to get in because she had a last-minute cancellation. Next appointment, I scheduled to have microneedling."

Megan's eyes widened. "But isn't that invasive? Maybe we should look into it a little more first."

Kate huffed. "You have the skin of a baby because, guess what, you are a baby. I hope all of that wasn't expensive because you wasted your money."

Kate immediately left the kitchen but Felicity followed her. "I was going to invite you to go out with us. Robin and I are taking her out tonight so that we can show her around but if you're going to be so negative about everything you can just forget about it. Robin and I will entertain Sasha by ourselves."

Nolan leaned against the kitchen counter, a dazed look on his face. "Did she just say that girl's name is Sasha?"

Megan nodded. "It was hard to tell between all the acids and the bleeding I was envisioning from the microneedling, but yes. She said her new friend's name is Sasha."

Luke was breathless as he ran into the kitchen. "Megan, you have to come with me right now.

Where's Kate? Get Kate too."

Megan followed Luke, who was still trying to catch his breath. He pointed out the living room window and Megan's hand flew to her mouth. "Oh, you'd better tell Chelsea too."

Nolan was right behind her, trying to see what had them so alarmed. Within seconds, everyone scattered like it was a fire drill. Luke ran to the kitchen and started moving the cases of wine to the veranda. Chelsea was clearing out all of the decanters from the bar and Felicity ran to her room, locking the door with a loud click.

Kate was on the floor, her face covered by both hands, trying to breathe through an anxiety attack. Megan was standing in front of the hallway mirror, calmly applying lipstick. They'd all run off, leaving Nolan alone at the window. He turned to see what had everyone in a panic.

A big yellow taxi sat outside, idling in front of the house. The driver got out and went to the rear of the taxi, opening the trunk and setting three pieces of matching white leather luggage on the ground. He waited and when no one came out of the house, he opened the car door.

White stiletto heels inched out and were followed by the long, lean lines of a young woman. A woman who looked more at home on a yacht than a farm. In sleek white pants with a matching jacket draped over her shoulders, a white bandeau top showed off her toned midriff. Her blonde hair was pulled back in a low smooth bun and a small dog was tucked under her arm.

She slowly pushed her sunglasses onto her head and surveyed her surroundings like she was there to either buy the place or burn it down.

She brought a tanned arm out from under her jacket and shaded her eyes, looked directly at Nolan, and smiled. He didn't know who she was but she'd just caught him shamelessly staring at her.

What's next...
Homecoming
Bristol Bay Book 2

Spend a fun and memorable summer at Bristol Bay when an uninvited and unexpected guest sweeps into Cove House, causing chaos among the close-knit cousins.

Is she here to buy the place or burn it down? Or maybe she plans on doing both. First, they have to find out where she's been and why she's here.

Felicity has to decide if she wants the man she's always loved or the man who treats her like a woman.

Kate continues to be the most secretive member of the family. Will anyone get her to open up before she cracks under the stress?

Megan Atwood and Nolan Prescott's relationship becomes interwoven with a parallel love story from one hundred years ago. When Megan exposes a secret that her great grandmother went to great lengths to keep, she uncovers a love story that runs as deep as the ocean and spans two shores for eternity. This tale of bittersweet love changes the way she sees everything.

If you like surprises and clean romance, you'll love this romantic women's fiction series where one family's saga portrays the strength of love and forgiveness.

Thank you for reading *Cove House*!
I hope you enjoyed it as much as I enjoyed
writing it.

Reviews mean so much to authors, I would
love it if you would consider leaving one.
Thank you so much for taking the time to
support me and my work!

About the Author

Christine Gordon is an American author who loves books, puppies, and chocolate. She's been telling stories her whole life and with the encouragement from friends and family, she decided to stop talking and start writing. You can find her with her nose in a book or throwing a ball for her three precious babies, BooBoo, Duckie and Teddy. She's also been known to hand out treats, something she'll deny when they're being weighed at their yearly check up!

Made in the USA
Columbia, SC
18 November 2021